REDEMPTION OF THIEVES

LEGENDS OF DIMMINGWOOD, BOOK IV

C. Greenwood

Copyright © 2013 C. Greenwood
Edited by Victory Editing
Formatted by Polgarus Studios
Cover art by Michael Gauss

ALL RIGHTS RESERVED. Excepting brief review quotes, this book may not be reproduced in whole or in part without the express written permission of the copyright holder. The unauthorized reproduction or distribution of this copyrighted work is illegal.

This is a work of fiction. Any resemblance to persons, living or dead, real events, locations, or organizations is purely coincidental.

A Beginning

I'm glad the path we follow edges the borders of Dimmingwood. Do the others take this route for my benefit? It seems like years since I've felt the soft earth of the forest floor beneath my feet, smelled the mingled scent of leaf mold and pine, and let the dappled sunlight and leaf patterns play across my face.

But I force myself to stick to the road, only looking on my home from a distance. I don't dare venture into the shadows. I tremble, even beneath the warm light of day and with strong companions at my side. Something dark calls to me from within that forest, a voiceless whisper inside my head. One I fear I don't have the strength to resist. The magic my ancestors bequeathed me throbs at the call of that other force, and I struggle to silence their pained cries in my mind. How long before I can wield my magic again without outside interference? I have no answers.

And so I heave a sigh, half-sorry and half-relieved as the road peels away from Dimming's borders and leads me in a new direction.

Chapter One

Immediately after being turned out of the Praetor's audience chamber, I was escorted away by a trio of Fists down the same corridors I'd passed through before. Even knowing I wasn't traveling toward death this time, my heart was heavy. I faced an even worse fate now. I'd become the Praetor's creature. And I didn't know who I despised more for it—my enemy or myself.

I wanted to believe I'd sworn the oath for Fleet's sake, but in my heart I wondered if that was true. Had I acted to protect my friend or to save my own life? Had I lost my nerve at the crucial moment?

I was scarcely aware of my surroundings as I passed down the long, empty corridors, my mind fully focused on what had transpired back in the audience chamber. I could still see the confused look on Fleet's face as his hands were bound and he was dragged away, protesting, between two Fists. Little had he known when he befriended me what a high cost he would pay for our association.

I shook the image from my head even as I became aware of a new set of footsteps adding itself to our number. One of my escorts saluted and moved aside to allow the newcomer to fall in beside me.

"Impressive," I remarked. "So you're commanding Fists these days? What was the price of your new promotion, Under-Lieutenant?"

Terrac said nothing, and I risked a glance at him.

"You've grown," I admitted grudgingly. "I almost didn't know you back there with the Praetor."

It was true. I was used to viewing my one-time friend as a boy, and it was disconcerting to realize he'd become a man since our last meeting. I wondered if I looked different to him too.

"I knew you easily enough," he said, as if following my thoughts.

"I'll bet you did. It's hard to forget the face of a friend you've betrayed."

He missed a step, abruptly dropping his confident demeanor. "I guess I figured by now you'd have grown up as much inside as out," he said. "My mistake."

I'd overpowered his newfound self-assurance in a single stroke, and sensing his annoyance, I couldn't help grinning.

"Whatever it is you've come to say to me, say it, priest boy. I've known you long enough to recognize the way you work your jaw when you've got something on your mind."

He frowned, glancing around. "Keep a civil tongue when you address me, woods thief."

I laughed. "By my greatmother, you always were a pompous little twit. You might have grown into a Fist's uniform and learned a trick or two with that shiny new sword at your side, but you haven't changed any more than I have."

I noticed the guards around us exchanging amused glances and was pleased my darts were hitting the mark.

I was startled when Terrac seized my arm and dragged me to a halt while snapping at his underlings, "Return to your duties. I'll escort her out."

"But, sir—" one protested.

"I said you are dismissed."

Even I had to admire the authority he put behind the command. If his men were a little slow to follow it, they moved away nonetheless.

"You shouldn't allow that," I warned when they were out of earshot. "Let them drag their steps on the little orders and they'll never respect you when the time comes for serious ones."

"Don't you suppose I know that?" he retorted. "Why do you think I sent them away? I can't have them hearing you talk down to me or, worst of all, let them see me permitting it. I'm fighting an uphill battle here, Ilan. I've yet to earn their respect. They still regard me as the orphaned woods brat who got a free leg up by having the right connections."

"Connections?" I scoffed. "What connections? You're a farmer's son from Cros. Not to make less of your fine history of command or the long years of experience behind you, but I confess their speculation is mine."

Ignoring the way his eyes narrowed at my sarcasm, I couldn't resist adding, "Just how did you manage it? You were always good at whining and scheming until you got what you wanted, but I don't remember you ever being especially ambitious in the old days."

"People change," he said stiffly. "I've realized what I want from life and have found the courage to pursue it."

"That wasn't my question, although it's an interesting one. I asked how you managed to obtain this *leg up*, as you call it. Who supplied the ladder?"

He looked uneasy. "Never mind. I can't talk about that. Just pay attention when I tell you not to mock me before my underlings. I put up with it today for old time's sake, but don't make it a habit."

"Aren't you forgetting something? I'm under the Praetor's protection now," I pointed out. "None of his lackeys have the power to lay a finger on me without his nod. So I think what you mean to say is that you *request* I show you proper deference before your peers. As a favor, no less."

He sighed. "Fine. Word it any way you like. I've no time for games, and this isn't what I came to discuss with you."

"Then why did you come to me? To salve your conscience for standing by while your lord imprisoned Fleet?"

He cut a sidelong glance at me. "What is this Fleet's fate to you? Is there some involvement I should know about?"

I shrugged. "He's just a friend. Even if he were more, that'd be no concern of yours, would it?"

He dodged the question. "Your friend will be treated well enough so long as he's cooperative, although it'd be no great loss to the world if he weren't. His list of crimes is long enough to stretch from here to the next province."

"I suppose you'd say the same about Kipp and the others? What excuse has your overworked conscience invented for allowing your master to string up your one-time friends?"

"They were your comrades, never mine," he answered, but I sensed a flicker of unease within him. "I was never party to your outlawry and was disgusted by the whole business. Don't make it sound as if they were innocents murdered for no wrongdoing. I assure you I had ample opportunity during my days in Dimming to observe acts vile enough to condemn every one of them."

"And is that what you did?" I asked, a sinking sensation burrowing deep in my belly as I imagined him witnessing against them.

"It wasn't like that," he hurried to assure me. "I could have spoken against them, but I didn't. At the end of the day, my testimony wasn't necessary."

I hid my relief, unsure why it mattered so much that he hadn't taken part in their fates.

He didn't allow me to take comfort for long, saying, "But I warn you, if the day ever comes when I must do my honest duty in that regard, I will. I won't carry out outlaw executions with any pleasure, but I'll do what the Praetor requires of me."

I blinked, remembering the gentle boy he had once been. "You've truly changed."

"If I have, it started with you. You're the one who saved me all those years ago, introduced me to the band of the Red Hand, and goaded me into fending for myself at the expense of others."

"I wouldn't say goaded."

"I would. You were always mocking me, challenging me to stand up for myself."

"Someone had to. You were pathetic."

He surprised me by smiling. "Yes, I was. But in a good way, I think."

He looked sadly reminiscent, as if mourning something forever lost. Then he shook his head. "Well, there's no use thinking of that. Obviously I was never meant for the priesthood. I've found my place now, although it might never have happened if not for the night Brig died. The night you picked up that bow. I see you're still carrying it."

I didn't stop him as he reached out to stroke the finely grained wood of the bow. I was getting used to peoples' strange attraction to the weapon, the way everyone's attention was eventually drawn to it.

"Maybe it's nonsense," he said, "but somehow I feel both our lives started changing after you found this thing. Almost like the bow started it all. You see how being with you again wakes strange ideas in my mind?"

I squirmed. "Any strange notions are your own. They're nothing to do with me or the bow."

"Maybe." He sounded unconvinced. "I don't suppose you'd ever consider giving it up?"

"What? The bow?"

"I don't blame you for being surprised. It's true I've never had any skill at shooting. But there's something about this weapon. I'd pay you well for it. Whatever you think it's worth."

I quelled the jealousy that stirred in me at the very thought of another person in possession of my bow.

I said, "You couldn't meet such a price. Anyway, it's not for sale. I'd die before parting with it."

I didn't realize until the words slipped out of my mouth how much I meant them.

"Die?" He raised his brows. "That's a strong statement. There aren't many things in this world worth dying for."

I shrugged. Under his scrutiny I was suddenly eager to be away. "I've been given my orders." I reminded him with a resentful emphasis on the last word. "I think I'd better waste no more time in carrying them out. It would grieve me to break my solemn oath to my new master on the first day." I turned away.

"Wait." He caught my arm, looking suddenly hesitant. "The reason I came after you is because I have something to say. It's about the last time we saw each other. Remember the night of our secret meeting in the water cemetery? I just want you to know I regret being so ungrateful back then. I was going through a difficult time, but that's no excuse, not when you risked so much to rescue me. I've often thought of it since."

"You've thought about me?" I asked. "I'm surprised you could find the time, what with a Fist's busy training schedule and the important new duties of an Under-lieutenant."

"Don't be so flippant. I'm trying to apologize."

"Then you're wasting your breath because you won't be forgiven."

"Look, we're both on the same side. We'll have to work together in the future."

That was enough to sap my stores of civility. "You and I," I said, "will never be on the same side of anything. Never again."

I'd made him angry, but it would take one who knew him well to see it. "Then who is on your side, Ilan? The great Rideon? I heard he cast you out."

"What do you know about that?" I hissed.

"The Praetor has his sources of information."

"You mean his spies? No doubt you have one or two planted among Rideon's men even now."

"Unfortunately, no. It was the captured criminals who told us so much. Your friend Kipp and the others."

I winced at the reminder. "If they confessed all they knew, why were they hanged? Didn't Kipp admit to being a member of my circle, one of those performing a valuable service to the Praetor and the Provinces?"

Terrac frowned. "You're trying to discover how much we know about your goings on in the forest. I'll be cooperative because I believe the Praetor wishes you to have the answer to this question. Your friends, when captured, have received and will continue to receive the same treatment as any other criminals, despite their recent good deeds for the province. My lord believes this will spur their determination to better perform the tasks ahead of them. You, their leader, are an exception because you must be permitted to come and go freely while reporting to the Praetor. But the rest of your unfortunate circle remain under the threat of death should they fall into our hands."

I swallowed my outrage to ask, "And suppose my friends refuse to accept these unfair terms?"

"Should they refuse to follow you into the Praetor's service, they ought to know this. Our lord is not a man to defy lightly. I know him well enough to assure you that if any of you were to mock him with a betrayal, he would make hunting down and destroying your band his greatest priority. Do not place too great a faith in your ability to evade his reach. He would throw every Fist and mercenary soldier he could muster into your dark woods until he had exterminated you to the last. You don't want to feel the fire of such a man's fury."

Little could he know I had felt it before. Images came to mind of a burning cottage, a line of horsemen riding down my father, my mama pressing a brooch into my hand…

I shoved the memories aside.

Terrac was saying, "But, there is no reason for despair. The Praetor is as merciful as he is vengeful, and if you do all he demands, pardons may be granted to those who merit them."

"Those who merit…?" I knew then that all of us were doomed. The Praetor would never give up his hold on us. We might spend countless years in servitude, and the Praetor would forever hold those pardons dangling over us.

I tried to set aside that problem for another day. My first task was to free Fleet, and I'd been advised of only one way to do that. Suddenly I had a thousand tasks on my mind, all of which needed to be carried out at once. I didn't realize I was walking away from Terrac without a word of good-bye until I came to the great brass-bound doors that led out of the keep. By the time I looked back, my one-time friend was gone.

It struck me then that I had failed to ask him the one question that had been teasing at the back of my mind throughout our encounter. Why was he wearing my brooch? The one my mother had given me so many years ago and which had disappeared from my possession when Terrac left Dimmingwood?

I couldn't imagine why he would have stolen the object, but of one thing I was sure. I wanted it back.

Chapter Two

Over the following week I reestablished contact with the remnants of the old circle through Kipp's brother, who had once been our messenger. It was essential to open the old lines of communication again because I had no other means of passing information between me and my comrades. Rideon's ban from Dimmingwood was still in effect, and I wasn't ready to risk his wrath yet.

I was painfully conscious of the balance I must keep between service to the Praetor and loyalty to my old band and its captain. With Rideon on one side and the Praetor on the other, to stumble would mean my death.

The Skeltai raiders were a more distant threat but every bit as real as the other two. There was also the unknown mage I had yet to unmask but whom I suspected of being the Praetor. My enemies were growing in number, and sorting foes from temporary allies grew more confusing by the day.

But one night I forgot all this. I was restless, lying in my cot aboard the river raft, where I was staying with my friend Hadrian. Every time I closed my eyes, memories rose unbidden to tickle the back of my mind. Memories of faces and voices I hadn't seen or heard in a long, long time. A dizzy sensation overtook me, and I smelled the scent of plum blossoms.

I opened my eyes and found myself atop a grassy green ridge. Looking down one side, a small village spread out before me in the waning evening light, smoke rising from the chimneys of the country cottages and chickens pecking around the yards. A deep calm pervaded the scene, and I felt it lap over me. I was at peace. I looked over the other side of the ridge, and there I saw a lonely cottage nestled in a shallow valley. There was a meadow of waving grass behind the cottage and a stand of trees leading into a forest fronting the farm. A dilapidated barn leaned near the house, a broken-down wagon out front. Inside a small enclosure nearby grazed a horse.

Drawn irresistibly toward the cozy little homestead, I traveled a lightly worn path down the ridge and into the valley, weaving in and out of a row of plum trees covered in pink blossoms and emitting a sweetly familiar scent.

The ground shifted under me and I found myself no longer on the path but approaching the front porch of the cottage. It didn't seem strange this should happen. Another shift and I was walking in the open door.

Everything around me was familiar, the room, the furnishings. The big bed in the middle of the room and the crackling fireplace over which something was cooking. I looked for my little bed tucked away in the corner, but it wasn't there. In its place stood a wooden cradle, and in that cradle something moved.

Approaching cautiously, I peered over the side and saw an infant only a few months of age lying amid a pile of thick, soft blankets knitted in a pattern I recognized as one of Mama's. The pale-skinned baby turned its head, which was covered in tufts of silvery hair, and looked up at me with solemn gray eyes. Somehow I knew I was looking at myself.

I felt no sense of alarm at what I was vaguely aware should be a startling turn of events. Somehow this, like everything else in this place, felt perfectly natural.

"Do you think she'll be safe here? Will any of us ever be safe again?"

I turned at the female voice.

I wasn't alone anymore but stood alongside a couple looking down on the baby. He was tall and dark bearded, she pale and silver-haired, her long tresses drawn back to reveal delicately pointed ears. It was startling to see Mama so young. Had she always looked like that? So much like... me?

Da put his arm around her. "Nothing can touch us here."

The sound of his well-remembered voice made my eyes sting.

"I'll make sure of that," he continued. "The villagers are mostly magickers, and they've accepted us. We'll be away from prying eyes in this place."

"But your family...," she protested.

"Are far away, and they don't know we have a child. Even if they did, what does it matter? I'm sure *his* anger has cooled by now—"

"You don't really believe that."

"If I thought otherwise, would I have settled us in the same province?" he asked.

She shook her head, as if she had heard this argument before. "You know how hot his anger is, how he hates my people, especially now that I've stolen you away. He swore to hunt us down after your abandonment, and he'll never rest until he does. Not while he believes you've betrayed him."

He smiled and kissed her neck gently. "I had to follow the bidding of my heart."

"But look what it's gotten you, at the danger it's placed us in. Yes, and maybe other magickers too. What has our selfish, reckless love done?"

Tears trickled out the corners of her eyes, and he moved to comfort her. Neither seemed aware of me. I was so near they might have reached out and touched me, but instead they looked through me as though I were a ghost.

Was I? Had I died in my sleep and wandered into some strange afterworld where I was forced to repeat scenes from my life, reliving each moment from the beginning, watching but never participating? And this was a scene from my life. I had no doubt about that. Somewhere in the distant past, this conversation had happened before.

For the first time I felt troubled, as if I were witnessing moments I wasn't meant to see. Not the grown me, anyway. The baby in the cradle saw all and looked on, unblinking.

I backed away, suddenly desiring to be somewhere, anywhere, else. The cottage felt close, the air oppressive. I thought I had come home, but I was wrong. This wasn't my home anymore. I shouldn't be here.

I was reminded forcefully of a time I had seen Brig shortly after his death. Had strayed into some gray memory of him where I'd felt briefly comforted before recognizing the wrongness of what was happening and pushing his flickering image away.

I pushed now and was swept up in a dizzying sensation, and the world around me shifted.

I awoke to find warm sunlight streaming over me and Seephinia cooking breakfast.

* * *

I told Hadrian about my nighttime visit to the home of my childhood.

"I have heard of such dreams," he told me. "Many magickers are prone to them, though I myself have never experienced one."

"It wasn't a dream," I said, unsure how I knew that. "It was real. Everything I heard and saw… at some point all of it really happened. I think I strayed into some sort of…" I hesitated, looking for a word to describe it.

"A magical rift," he supplied.

"A what?"

"A tear in the fabric of time and possibly of distance as well. There are rumors such things exist, but again, I've had no personal experience with them."

"I think I've experienced one of these *rifts* before," I said and told him about the occasion after Brig's death when I had seen a vision of my friend.

"At the time I thought I was losing my mind or seeing a ghost," I finished. "But now I realize it felt the same as what happened last night. Like I was truly seeing Brig in a real moment of his life. Maybe even from a time before I knew him."

"It's possible," Hadrian agreed. "I suppose we'll never know the truth. Not unless you think you can stumble into one of these rifts again. Can you?"

I thought about it. "I don't think so. It's not something I can control. Both times it's happened, it just came over me suddenly. I didn't seek it out."

"Not consciously anyway," he suggested.

I didn't want to think about that. My conscious mind had enough to deal with right now without worrying about what mischief my subconscious was up to.

I changed the subject and suggested we go out fishing with Seephinia's young nephew, Eelus.

* * *

I didn't have long to brood over my new discovery of magical rifts.

The following day a distraction came in the form of a visitor showing up on our doorstep. The old peasant hag, dressed in a baggy skirt with a frayed shawl drawn over her head, was peddling tin pots. She was the tallest old woman I'd ever seen. Even with her shoulders hunched, she towered over Seephinia in the doorway.

When the ruckus began, I was at the back of the hut, poring with Hadrian over an old map of the Dark Forest I had procured from a traveling fur trader passing through Selbius the day before. I wasn't sure why I had taken up the idea to study the lay of the Skeltai lands but felt it couldn't hurt my position to know my enemy's home ground. The map was shriveled and worn, drawn out on a bit of cured hide, and I had only the word of the trader that any of it was an accurate portrayal of what lay on the other side of the provincial border. I suspected the villages and habitations marked on the map were outdated and so focused my attention on landmarks, committing them to memory. Hills, lakes, and forests didn't change much over the course of years.

I was dimly aware of Seephinia at the door arguing with someone but paid scarce attention until their quarreling grew louder. Annoyed, I looked up from the map spread over a low table to find the source of my distraction.

The ragged old woman in the doorway bore a long stick across her broad, crooked shoulders from which dangled a collection of rusted and dented pots and pans.

Even as she disputed with the river woman in a reedy, high-pitched voice, she shoved her way into the hut.

Seephinia's face darkened dangerously as she protested in the tongue of the river folk, but the old peddler wasn't to be dissuaded.

"Look here, old mother," Hadrian interrupted, hurrying to settle the argument, "we appreciate the quality of your excellent goods, but I'm afraid we have no need of pots or pans at present."

Ignoring him, the old woman slung closed the curtain over the doorway and let her collection of wares fall to the floor with a clatter.

Seephinia sputtered in indignation but Hadrian held her back. "Perhaps you didn't understand me," he tried again.

His words cut off abruptly as the old woman straightened to her full height and threw back the hood of her shawl to reveal a mane of wild, red hair over a youthful male face. Ridged scars zigzagged his cheeks, but the disguised man's lips were drawn back into a familiar grin.

I sprang to my feet. "Dradac! How did you get here? Who told you where to find me?"

He laughed. "You left instructions for reaching you with Kipp's brother. As to the how, you see that for yourself. No one looks long at a cantankerous old peasant woman selling a load of dented crockery."

I tried to be stern. "Those instructions were for emergencies, Dradac. I expressly forbade anyone but the messenger to risk coming here in person. If you want me to remain leader of the circle, you must pay attention to my orders. Terrac's Fists obey him better than any of my followers listen to me."

He looked confused. "Terrac's Fists?"

I had never explained to Dradac and the rest of my outlaw friends the connection between Terrac and the Praetor's soldiers, and I wasn't about to now. "Never mind. Just don't do this again," I growled.

"Maybe it will relieve your concern if I tell you I'm acting in accordance with your orders even now," he said. "It's nothing less than an emergency that brings me here. A Skeltai scout was seen materializing near the woods settlement along Beaver Creek."

"Materializing?" Hadrian stepped in.

"It's a magical method of travel used by the Skeltai raiders and their shaman," I explained hastily. "No one knows how they do it. Go on, Dradac."

"Our man followed instructions," he continued. "He held back and observed long enough to see the scout circle the settlement several times before pulling his disappearing trick again."

"You think they're marking the place in advance of a raid?" I asked. "You're probably right. It fits their usual pattern. I'll pass the word to the Praetor, and he'll have his men stationed there to stave off an attack before it comes."

"Not so fast. I want to discuss an idea with you. That's why I came directly instead of sending the messenger. I believe the Skeltai mean to attack this very night. Ada tells us tonight is a special occasion for her people—the final rites of Sagara Nouri."

I bolted upright at mention of the pagan holiday. "I'm listening."

"Good. We decided the purpose of the raids was to appease their gods by gathering sacrificial victims for their festival, right?" So it occurs to me, tonight being the bloodiest night of their rituals, Beaver Creek is likely to be their greatest massacre."

"Not if we act quickly," I said. "With the Praetor's men surrounding the settlement, we may prevent the attack and drive the Skeltai back. It's worked before."

"But this is my idea… What if the Fists weren't to show up so speedily? What if they held back and waited for the Skeltai raiders to make the first move? I know we've tried trapping them before—"

"You're rotting right it's been tried before," I cut him off. "More than once too. But the enemy always discovers our presence too soon, and they disappear before we can close in."

"Only because we were impatient," he argued. "But this time, let's hold back our Fists until the raiders have engaged with the villagers. They'll be unable to extricate themselves and flee as we come charging in."

"Meanwhile villagers will be slaughtered for some minutes while we're too far away to do them any good," I pointed out.

But he wouldn't be swayed. "Balance their deaths against the number of lives that may be saved by this plan.

Rather than counter one attack after another, wouldn't you rather stop the Skeltai permanently?"

"I don't see how that's going to happen."

"Just listen. What if we got close enough through the method of surprise to arrive while the raiders' magic portal is still open? We could send our men through the portal after their retreating army and trace them back to their home ground."

"You want to strand a handful of men deep in enemy territory with an overwhelming number of enemies and no possible means of return?"

He rubbed his chin. "I wouldn't suggest a handful. Make it a large enough party to do some damage. Let us show them we're capable of striking back. Maybe it'll put a little fear into them if we prove we aren't going to remain helpless victims. I can't swear this would put a stop to their raids, but if we show an ounce of their own cunning, they might learn to respect us as a force to be reckoned with."

I frowned. "There may be something to the idea. At any rate, I'll certainly bring it up to the Praetor. All decisions are up to him. But I wouldn't count on anything coming of it, if I were you. It's a suicide mission. It might make a statement to the enemy, but the fact remains no one entering that portal is likely ever to set eyes on home again. Even if our people miraculously won their battle with the Skeltai on the other side of the portal—and that's assuming the savages don't have superior numbers on hand to replace their warriors as they fall—there are still days or weeks of travel ahead of any survivors. We have no way of knowing the distance between wherever the portal lets out and the borders of the province. It'd be rough to cover enemy territory on foot, even for someone who knows his way through the Dark Forest. And I'm not sure such a guide is to be found. Certainly not in the little time we have."

"Ada could do it," he suggested. "And of course I'd go too."

"No," I said sharply. "I've lost too many friends lately. I can count the number of loved ones remaining to me on the fingers of one hand and have digits left over. No one is going through that portal unless it's the Praetor's Fists. He can throw away as many of his soldiers as he wishes, but I won't let him waste my people on this. Anyway, Ada hasn't been on the other side of the border since she was a child. I think she overestimates her ability to lead a band of men, many of them likely injured, back home again."

He frowned. "I think you're *under*estimating Ada. She's not one to accept failure, and I'd be there to prop her up. She'd get us home one way or another."

"Enough. I've already said no, and I don't mean to change my mind." I rose and snatched up my bow from its place on the wall. "Now I've got a message to deliver up at the keep. Our time grows short."

He walked me to the door. "Will you be accompanying the Fists?"

"Not likely. You know Rideon doesn't permit my presence in Dimmingwood." I couldn't hide the trace of bitterness in my voice.

He nodded, but there was a distant look in his eyes. I wondered what he was planning.

* * *

At the keep I was shown into a dark-paneled room I had never seen before and instructed to await the Praetor's convenience. Fully aware a guard was posted outside the door, it never occurred to me to do anything else, although the idea of passing interminable minutes in this stuffy little room while I carried such vital information was frustrating.

I controlled my impatience by studying my surroundings. It was a crowded but carefully organized room, dominated by a large elderwood desk at the center and a high-backed chair. Floor-to-ceiling shelves lined the walls, most of them filled with leather-bound books or stacks of scrolls. I was surprised to recognize one object displayed on the shelves. My knife. It was the very one I had so recently used in my attack on the Praetor, although the blade was now polished to a sheen and bore no remaining trace of blood or poison.

I scowled. It was in keeping with the arrogant nature of my enemy to keep and display like a prize the weapon of his would-be assassin.

I continued to scan the shelves. There were a few foreign instruments I didn't recognize arranged among the books, such as a large, revolving ball on a stand with multicolored patches and markings covering the surface. Small writing was scrawled across the ball and, peering closer to make it out, I realized I was looking at a map of the provinces and surrounding areas stretched over a globe. I'd never seen anything like it before.

I turned my attention from the objects on the shelves to the tidy arrangement on the desktop. An inkpot, blotter, and quill stood on the right side where the hand would naturally fall, and stacked next to these were a few clean sheets of parchment. At the other side of the desk was spread a clumsy heap of scrolls, and in the center stood a candle stand holding a cold stub of wax, mostly melted away.

As I circled around behind the desk, I couldn't help thinking what a perfect opportunity this was. Almost too perfect. Could the Praetor have some ulterior motive for leaving me alone in this room? Something he wanted me to find? I dismissed the thought as a ridiculous one. Why should the man *want* me to riffle through his desk? For another moment I held back, studying the silver-knobbed drawers longingly. Then I cast a cautious glance over my shoulder and gave in to temptation. I had vowed to obey the Praetor, it was true, but I was fairly certain he'd never specifically commanded me not to snoop through his things.

I ducked behind the desk and slid open the upper drawer on the right-hand side. Nothing. Some extra sheets of parchment, more stoppered pots of ink, and a slender book. I picked it up and flipped through the pages, but it contained nothing of interest. A shower of pressed flower petals and leaves slipped from between the pages as I turned them, and I replaced the sprigs with some amusement before putting the book back into the drawer. I wouldn't have thought the Praetor the sort for collecting sentimental mementos.

The second drawer held a thick sheaf of papers. I only had time to scan a handful, but they all seemed to be ancient notes on the history of the Skeltai race and the use of magic in the provinces in the days before the land became settled and most of my Skeltai ancestors had been driven out. That was surprising since the Praetor was so adamantly opposed to magickers. Why should he study a people and a practice he hated?

I spent little time on the next drawer as it only contained more dried plants, this time chopped into bits or preserved whole in jars. As I glanced over them, I noticed a stoppered bottle filled with a reddish liquid resembling dried blood. Another vial, half-empty, contained some blackish substance I didn't want to guess the origins of. A peculiar smell of decay emitted from this collection, and I moved on quickly. It was in the bottom left drawer that I eventually made a discovery in the form of a delicate, silver-worked box. There was a pretty little lock on the lid, but I would be a poor thief indeed if I didn't carry a lock-pick and know how to use it. I took care not to damage the lid or the lock, and in moments, I had the box open. Its contents gazed up at me.

A feeling of unreality settled over me, for looking up at me was a familiar face miniaturized in a framed portrait small enough to fit in the palm of my hand. Before I knew what I was doing, I was holding the miniature. I almost didn't know my own Da. Indeed, I wouldn't have known him if his face hadn't been fresh in my mind after my recent dream. He was young here, perhaps no more than twenty, and more finely dressed than I had ever seen him. There was a wistful look around his eyes and a solemn cast to his clean features. It must have required a skilled artist to capture him so perfectly. The kind of portraitist a farmer of dubious origins should never have been able to afford. Who had commissioned this likeness, and more importantly, how had it fallen into the Praetor's hands? Was it part of some plan to control me? Had he been researching my family history?

I scrambled to make sense of this finding. I couldn't reconcile my memories of my gruff father with his weathered face and work-callused hands to the image of this cultured-looking youth with his smooth chin and courtier-style clothing.

Suddenly I heard a door creaking open, and I scrambled out from behind the desk, whipping the miniature portrait behind my back. It was only the guard who'd been posted outside the door, peering in to see what mischief I might be up to. I shrugged and tried to look nonchalant. I must have appeared more innocent than I felt, because after a cursory glance around the room, the man pulled his head back out and the door was closed again.

I realized then I had better use more care. It might just as easily have been the Praetor coming in to catch me with his portrait—no, *my Da's* portrait—in my hands. I reluctantly returned the miniature to the box. I hated to do that as I had hated nothing before or since vowing obeisance to the Praetor, but I had little choice. Even with the pained and confused emotions the sight of the portrait awakened within me, I still had enough mental clarity to know I must keep the Praetor from discovering I had found it.

I hastily relatched the box, replacing it in the bottom drawer. I checked to be certain everything else I had touched was back in its proper place and then abandoned the desk and pulled up a high-backed chair in the corner to await whatever happened next.

Time seemed to drag by, but as there were no windows in the room through which to judge the changing shadows, I had no way of knowing if I had truly been waiting for hours or if it was my own guilt and sense of urgency that made it seem so.

I fell again to looking round the room. My eyes were drawn to the only untidy aspect of the place and the heap of scrolls I had vaguely noticed before spread out on the desk. They were disarranged and jumbled, looking as though they had been searched through with clumsy haste by the room's last occupant before being shoved aside. One I noted had tumbled to the floor and been left to lie at the foot of the desk. Automatically I stretched from my chair and bent to retrieve the fallen scroll. As I set it on the edge of the desk, my eyes fell upon another scroll, unrolled and held open by a heavy rock weight.

Curious, I bent over it and tried to make out the cramped writing scrawled across the page. There were words I was unfamiliar with, but it seemed to be some sort of recipe, a detailed list of herbal ingredients and the proper ways to mix them. What was it the Praetor found so fascinating in plants and dried dead things?

I found a second sheet behind the first, and on it were drawn detailed sketches of various plants with descriptions underneath. I paused as I recognized one of the herbs from Javen's lessons. I had never heard the fancy name titled beneath the sketch, but we knew it as horse clover. It had no healing properties I was aware of beyond offering a questionable relief for sour stomach. For some reason, however, the five-petal flower held my attention. Now I thought of it, I was fairly sure that had been horse clover petals I found pressed in the book inside the Praetor's desk.

What was it Javen had told me about horse clover? Some superstitious folk would never touch the plant, not even for medicinal purposes, because a certain dark influence was associated with it. It was said in the days when sorcery was common and magic used openly among the people, in that "evil" time before the Praetor had purged our part of the Province of this magical pestilence, that such plants as horse clover, black fern, and bitterweed were used commonly among practitioners of magic as components for the casting of spells. Most folk, of course, lumped magickers into the one general category, as I had before Hadrian had taught me of mages and naturals. A natural, I knew, would have no need of spells or their components.

I frowned at the implications of my find. Could the Praetor be studying the arts of magery? Or was there some other purpose for these lists and sketches? Perhaps a simple interest in botany? Certainly I had always found the study of plants and herbs interesting under Javen's tutelage. But it seemed too much of a coincidence that I should find these things in the Praetor's keeping in addition to all the other causes he had given me for suspicion.

I considered the jars of suspicious substances in his desk drawers and the notes I had found on ancient magic. I thought back to his miraculous recovery after being stabbed with my poisoned blade. Any ordinary man should have died, yet he massaged the wound and muttered strange incantations under his breath and suddenly it was as if the poison had never entered his blood.

I remembered how he had taken my tainted blade and slipped it into his robes. My eyes went again to my polished knife resting in a place of prominence on the shelf. His wanting to take the knife before anyone else had the chance to examine it suddenly made sense. He didn't want it to be proved that there truly was poison on the blade or there would be questions as to how he had survived without even growing sick. It wouldn't do, I supposed, for his underlings to uncover the secret. To realize the man himself dabbled in the very magic he condemned in others.

I raged inwardly. Suddenly my mother's and father's murders seemed all the more needless and insane now I knew the man who had ordered them practiced the same forbidden magic in a different form. I also saw now that my attempt at assassination must have been a source of great amusement to my enemy, armed as he was with power against such weak efforts.

I remembered Terrac's miraculous healing from that arrow shaft between the shoulder blades so long ago. His incredibly quick recovery made sense now. So also did his attempt to protect the mage who had been responsible for his healing. The Praetor had much to lose should his strange secret come out, and Terrac was being coerced or perhaps simply guilted into keeping it.

It occurred to me I now held an excellent card for blackmailing purposes. At the same time I realized should the Praetor become aware I possessed such damning information against him he would snuff me out like a candle and with as little thought. My usefulness in the Skeltai matter stood as nothing next to the danger of allowing me to live.

"Perusing my papers, I see. Find anything of interest?"

I hadn't heard the door open. I whirled guiltily at the familiar voice, thinking that somehow my very thoughts must have conjured up the Praetor. He regarded me with disapproval tinged with cruel amusement. Remembering I still clutched the papers, I set them back on the desk and arranged the rock weight to pin them as I had found them, careful all the while to keep my actions slow and casual. If I hadn't already betrayed my guilt by holding the very papers in question, I would not do so now by showing fear.

"Fascinating sketches you have here," I said, surprised at the lightness of my tone. "I recognize a few of the plants. I've an interest in botany myself. Nothing like yours, maybe, but I've experimented with herbal cures and folk remedies."

"No doubt. You needn't be so modest in the face of my imagined expertise. I assure you I'm little more than an amateur." He crossed the room as he spoke and sank into the great chair behind his desk. "I dabble. Nothing more."

I saw him studying the arrangement of his desktop as if weighing what might be amiss. I kept speaking more from need to distract him than actual interest in the conversation.

"Now it is you who are being modest. Your talents must be advanced indeed to have afforded a recovery like yours after that brush with the poisoned blade."

I grimaced at my thoughtless words, as we both glanced at the knife in its place of prominence. Why could I not help goading my enemy, even at the moment when I could least afford to do so? His gaze returned to me, and I felt him studying me for some indication that my words carried any deeper meaning.

Something cold brushed at the front of my consciousness. It was not the familiar comforting presence of the bow. This was an alien presence, sinister and intrusive. In an instant, I threw up my mental walls and sealed them tight.

The Praetor smiled.

He knows. I couldn't discern whether the thought was mine or came from the bow but it scarcely mattered. He did know. Then came the frantic question. *What exactly does he know?*

I tried to remember what thoughts had been at the forefront of my mind when I had felt that cold questing. His secret, his magery. How could I hide my knowledge of that? This was all I had been dwelling consciously on at the time. I dared to hope all other secrets were safe. Not that it mattered. This one alone was enough to kill me.

I was faintly surprised when the Praetor said, "I required no herbal remedies. As I said earlier, the blade contained no toxins. You must have been mistaken in that. Your herbalist lied to you in order to make a sale."

He spoke easily, as if there had been no invisible exchange between us just now. I was too confused by his lack of reaction to argue that I was positive of my poison, that I had purchased a kind with which I was familiar. Besides, it was a dangerous line to pursue.

Luckily he seemed content to let the matter go, leaning back in his seat and turning his attention to the doorway. "Where is my captain? He should have been here by now. He knows better than to keep me waiting."

As if summoned by his very naming, the man appeared. "You summoned me, my lord?"

"Yes. The thief girl has what she claims to be some highly important information to share with us." His tone was disparaging, but I wasn't fooled. If he didn't believe my message a matter some urgency, he would not be here now with the captain of his personal guard.

I lit into a full explanation of what I knew, including Dradac's suspicions on the timing of the eminent attack. I added, though no one asked, that in my opinion his supposition was well-founded. I said haste was advisable.

No one seemed to pay that recommendation any mind. As they began conferring on their next course of action, both men shut me out of the conversation as if my part in this matter were finished. Perhaps it was. Circumstances had arranged themselves to make me little more than a messenger. Who needed my advice or sought it?

The Praetor caught me as I was about to back out of the room. "Going somewhere, are you, Hound?"

"Yes. I thought if my business here was finished I might withdraw. My lord." I added that last with reluctance, but add it I did. After all, I had made a vow, hadn't I?

"I will tell you when your work is finished," he said. "For now, hurry and get yourself to the stables and order my horse saddled and prepared. And get yourself an animal while you're down there."

I blinked. "A horse for me, sir?"

The Praetor's captain spoke at the same time. "Your horse, lord? You will be accompanying the men when we ride out?"

The Praetor said, "To both your questions, yes and yes. I've yet to see in action these Skeltai who have the impudence to invade my lands. Who knows? If I am present, perhaps this time something will get done."

The Fist captain looked offended. "With all respect, my lord, I am certain I have always carried out your orders to the measure—"

I cut him off. I had my own questions, no less urgent than his. "Where am I going that I need a horse?"

The Praetor said to his underling, "Enough, Captain Delecarte. I have made my wishes known."

To me he said, "You'll be accompanying us, of course. We'll make better time with a guide to lead our force to this Beaver Creek. You're familiar with the terrain, are you not?"

As if either of us were going to forget my connection with Dimmingwood.

I said, "I'm afraid you forget one minor detail, sir. I've been banned from Dimming on pain of death."

"Oh? I hadn't heard of it. By whom?" His response was vague. He had turned his back on both of us and was riffling through some papers on his desk.

"By Rideon, the outlaw captain," I said.

"Ah yes, the notorious brigand leader. I haven't heard his name in some time. Most people's thoughts are too consumed with you."

"With me, sir?"

"Never mind. Well, what are you afraid of? You'll have an army at your back. I don't imagine this infamous rascal is capable of plucking you from our midst, do you? Consider yourself well protected."

Protected by Fists. Now that was a turn of events I had never expected to see coming.

As I excused myself and hurried out the door, I tried not to think of what sort of treason my old captain would construe if he heard of me passing through his territory with an army of Fists at my back.

Chapter Three

A half hour later, I was surprised to discover Terrac among those we would be riding out with. I had the opportunity to speak to him briefly as we and a party of Fists waited on horseback in the outer bailey for the Praetor to make his appearance.

I was full of my own worries about the excursion ahead, and the Praetor's reassurances had done little to relieve my anxiety. A hundred Fists behind me or not, I still wasn't confident I was beyond Rideon's wrath should he discover I was trespassing on his land. I had, after all, an advantage over the Praetor in this regard. I knew Rideon well. Well enough to know he was proud, vengeful, and clever enough to carry out what other men might consider impossible.

And I had other cause for discomfort. I had never been surrounded by so many Iron Fists before. Hemmed in on all sides by the black and crimson uniforms, I felt the sweat standing out on my forehead and a nervous clenching in the pit of my belly. I only hoped none of these louts got overly enthusiastic in the middle of the fighting and forgot I was on their side now.

As if sensing my nervousness, my horse, a heavy-footed animal with all the agility of an ox, shifted beneath me and shook his head testily. Naturally, I had been given the ugliest and most ill-trained creature in the stables. A glance at the ground, which felt a mile below me, reminded me I had rarely been on a horse. I'd never needed to learn anything about riding. It now struck me as an appalling omission on my part. It was ridiculous that I, who had fought both Fists and Skeltai in the thick of battle without so much as a quiver of fear, should be shaking in my boots at the prospect of a long ride on the back of a strange horse.

While all this was running through my mind, I became vaguely aware of a familiar presence tugging at the edge of my senses. I had mostly taken to keeping my barriers up at all times around the keep for fear of another surprise attack from my magic-wielding enemy, and I inwardly cursed myself for allowing my focus to slip. I would have to be extra cautious now that the Praetor realized—or at least I was nearly certain he realized—that I knew him to be that mage.

But this time it wasn't the Praetor who approached. It was only Terrac, drawing a muscled gray horse up alongside me. I couldn't help eyeing his sleek, smart-stepping animal with envy, and my own mulish beast shifted in agitation again as though he were sensing my thoughts and resentful of them.

Terrac said, "You're gripping too tight with your knees while hauling back on the reins at the same time. It's confusing him."

I ignored his unsought advice and tightened both holds grimly. "Thanks for the warning," I said. "But if I wanted an instructor, I'd take lessons. Anyway, if I wasn't holding on for my life, this cursed animal would already have me in the dust."

"No, he wouldn't. Old Snapper's not a bad mount. He just has to have confidence in the rider on his back. Convince him you aren't afraid of him and that you know what he's about, and he'll cut out his tricks."

"Tricks? He's got tricks?" I couldn't keep the dread from my voice. I had thought the shifting and stamping were all I had to worry about.

"Oh, he's got a whole bagful. But don't worry. Luckily for you, he's the same horse they gave me to train on, so I can tell you what to watch out for. Mostly, beware the teeth when he tosses his head back. Sometimes he does that right before he tries to get 'em clamped into your thigh. You'll also want to watch him particularly close when we get into the woods. He likes to scrape new riders off when he gets the chance, so don't let him get you too close to the trees."

"Great," I grumbled. As if I didn't have enough to worry about, even my own horse was out for my blood.

"You'll do all right," Terrac reassured me. "Just pretend you know what you're doing. That shouldn't be too hard for you. You were never short on confidence in the old days."

"Are you implying I pretended expertise at anything I couldn't handle?" I asked.

"Admit it. You were more egotistical than excellent when it came to our old sword lessons with Dradac. Mind you, I'm not saying you were incompetent—"

My face warmed. As I recalled, I'd usually come out on the winning end of our practice matches. I said, "Listen, priest boy, I'll cross swords with you and best you any time you feel like being humiliated in front of your new friends. Just name the time and place."

My challenge was interrupted by a commotion around us. The surrounding soldiers erupted into cheers, and my horse started nervously at the noise. It was a moment before I could get him under control again, and when I did, I looked around angrily for the cause of the stir. The Fists were chanting something I couldn't decipher and banging their gauntleted fists onto their metal breastplates, the result a discordant din painful to the ears but altogether effective as an attention getter.

I leaned half out of my saddle, which Snapper didn't care for much at all, to see my way past the crowd. Then the cause of the stir was evident. The Praetor was entering the bailey mounted on a coal-black war-steed, his captain and first lieutenant flanking him on either side. I gathered by his men's reaction his presence on such an occasion wasn't routine, but there was no doubt they were pleased to have him here to lead them.

Even I had to suppress a streak of admiration for the lord outfitted in the colors of blood and night and in armor more elaborate than that of his Fists. With his still, dark hair slicked back into a long tail and a great sword at his side, he looked much as he had the first time I saw him a dozen or more years ago. For an instant, I was transported back to that time, crouching among the rocks under the blazing sun and spying down on the man who would be Praetor one day. I shook my head to clear it of the image, and as the Praetor neared and the thin streaks of gray at his temples and shallow lines on his face became more apparent, it was easier to remind myself I was in a different time and place now.

The cheers fell into respectful silence. Captain Delecarte shouted a command, and the words had scarcely left his mouth before the Fists hurried to form themselves into ordered ranks. I had all I could do to guide my mount out of their way and attach myself to the side of their parade. I disrupted their pretty formation that way, but I had no desire to connect myself with them any more than I must. If I was commanded to accompany them, I would, but I had no intention of appearing to be a part of the Praetor's admiring hordes.

As for the great man himself, he took his place at the head of the lines with Delecarte and his officers. I was taken by surprise to see Terrac joining them. I kept forgetting he was under-lieutenant. He looked oddly out of place among the older, more seasoned fighting men. Again I wondered why the Praetor had favored him with such a position. I settled back and got as comfortable as I could on the back of the fiendish animal beneath me, preparing for a long and unpleasant ride.

* * *

Twilight filtered through the overhead canopy of Dimmingwood, and a chorus of frogs somewhere in the distance interrupted the stillness of approaching evening. I lay with my face against the cold earth and tried to ignore the many sticks and sharp rocks pressing into me. After hours in the saddle, every part of my body ached, and I carried a row of teeth marks across the thigh of my leather breeches where Snapper had lived up to his name on the ride here, much to the amusement of my companions.

Sucking in the crisp evening air tinged with the scent of earth and elder trees, I reminded myself I was on my home ground now. My enemies could mock me on theirs, but they had made equal fools of themselves since entering Dimmingwood, crashing through every tree and bramble bush in their path with enough noise to wake a graveyard. If not for me guiding them onto the proper paths, they would have ridden around in circles until morning and never come any closer to their destination.

I shook my head and tried to imagine away the three Fist scouts sprawled to either side of me in the deep grass, spying down on the tiny community settled at the edge of Beaver Creek. I could've operated so much better with my own familiar circle of thieves at my back rather than a reconnaissance party made up of men I still thought of as enemies. A horse whickered softly somewhere in the distance, reminding me the Praetor and his cursed Delecarte, along with the main body of men, waited only a short distance away, despite my advice to the contrary. No wonder the sleepy little village below showed no sign of activity other than the motions of the oblivious woodsfolk going about their evening routines. It would be a miracle if the Skeltai showed themselves at all with our presence so ill concealed.

At a sudden movement behind me, I whirled, expecting to find Skeltai warriors charging on us. Instead I saw one of the Fists who had been dispatched with me rolling around on the ground, wrestling with a large dark shadow in brown woods garb. The bigger stranger seemed to have gotten the better of our man, but the other two Fists were advancing on the struggling pair, swords already half-drawn. I shushed and waved them back, but they paid no heed to the commands, so I was forced to leap up and throw myself on top of the wrestlers, tumbling us all to the ground, to prevent the Fists slicing the newcomer's head off. When I rolled to my feet and got a look at our attacker, who still had the unfortunate Fist's head locked in his arms, I froze. My Fist companions didn't. They rushed at the man, and I scrambled to my feet to hold them back.

"Wait! Wait!" I said. "This man is one of ours. He's with me."

The Fists exchanged incredulous looks, but at least I had given them pause. I took a firmer stance. "This man is one of those forest thieves you've no doubt heard of who work under my command. He's a servant of the Praetor now, and your lord will be highly displeased if any harm befalls him."

I actually wasn't at all sure of that statement. The Praetor had plainly said I was the only one of my circle exempt from the penalties of law. But I was betting no one would go running back just now to ask him. Slowly, reluctantly, the Fists sheathed their blades.

Dradac's teeth flashed white in the gathering darkness. "Much obliged to you fellows. I was just stepping over to check in with my superior here, but this one got a little overenthusiastic when I startled him."

Releasing his hold on the head of the Fist, he crawled to his feet. I seized his elbow the moment I could be confident he wasn't about to be run through by the others and dragged him off to one side. With a cautious glance toward Beaver Creek to satisfy myself we had attracted no notice, I squatted in the grass, pulling him down beside me.

"What are you doing here?" I hissed. "I didn't tell you to interfere."

He grinned. "Ah, but you didn't tell me not to either, did you? I thought you could use some trustworthy company. Anyway, the question wasn't up to me. I couldn't hold Ada and the others back."

"Others? You don't mean to tell me there are more of the band out there?"

I peered into the trees at his back.

"Well, there's only Ada and a couple of new recruits, but I figured, with so many Fists surrounding you, you'd be happy for any help at all."

I frowned. "Haven't I told you the Praetor's protection doesn't extend to the rest of you? You shouldn't have changed the plan without warning me." His expression was unrepentant, and after a pause, I had to shrug. "The Praetor's unpredictable, it's true. For all I know he may be glad of the extra help. Then again, he might decide to haul you all back to Selbius and hang the lot of you. You'd be wise to get out of here while you can. At least go talk it over with the others."

But Dradac was stubborn. "We've talked it over, and we're staying."

I sighed. "Stay if you will then, but keep to the shadows unless I call you. If the Skeltai attack here tonight, the Fists will get so stirred up I'm not sure they'll know friend from foe."

He didn't like it. "We didn't come out here to duck around behind trees and watch the rest of you do the fighting."

"I won't be fighting either," I told him. "I'm just here as a guide and scout—a duty I'm making a poor job of at the moment, thanks to you."

I cast another glance over my shoulder at the village in the distance.

"When trouble starts, I'll stand back with the rest of you and let the Fists do what they do best."

When he still hesitated, I gave him a little shove in the direction of the trees. "Go on. Get out of here. Truth to tell, you're in my way just now."

I said it kindly but it was true. I had a task at hand, and he was a distraction.

My friend complied without further argument, and I returned to my post. Together the three Fists and I kept up our watch long into the evening. It wasn't until the night was blacker than pitch, the inhabitants of the village below had turned into their beds, and the singing of the tree frogs in the surrounding woods had faded that the Skeltai struck.

Chapter Four

One moment there was dead stillness in the little village below. The next, dark figures burst suddenly from the surrounding trees to swarm across the clearing. The Fist next to me started and cursed. We had seen no sign of scouts circling the village, no movement from within the shadows until the moment the Skeltai warriors appeared as if from nowhere. I was taken less by surprise than the other men in my company for I had the advantage of having seen the Skeltai in action before. I had scarcely hoped for any warning before the attack commenced.

I seized the nearest man by the elbow, never taking my eyes from the scene below. "Go back and alert the others. It's time to move in."

I signaled another of the soldiers. "You go with him. Keep a sharp eye to the trees."

Both men followed my orders without hesitation and ducked into the shadows, leaving me alone with the remaining Fist. Together we watched the horde of Skeltai swarm over the tiny village below.

My muscles tensed as the enemy broke over the neat row of darkened cabins like a tidal wave, and I had to force myself to remain where I hid. If they were alerted to our presence now, they might retreat before the trap was sprung. But it was a hard thing to do as I listened to the Skeltai's war cries and the splintering sounds of cabin doors being crashed open.

The Fist crouched in the grass beside me half rose, hand on sword hilt, as the screams of the villagers filled the night. Reading his intent, I dove for him and hauled him back down. It was fortunate he didn't resist because he was a burly fellow and I wouldn't have had the strength to match him. We remained helpless witnesses to the nightmarish scene unfolding before us.

I saw the destruction of the village, the innocent folk being driven half asleep from their beds. Those who attempted resistance were slaughtered in their tracks, and I found myself taken back to that night when the Skeltai had attacked Hammond's Bend. I was there all over again, feeling the horror and outrage as I watched frightened men and women fleeing for the cover of the trees before being run down and killed before my eyes.

A dark, subtle whisper chanted in the back of my mind now as it had done then, ever thirsty for blood. My bow seemed to burn through the cloth on my back, and almost unthinking, I slipped it off my shoulder. My fingers moved to take an arrow from my quiver. Realizing what I was doing, I hesitated a second. The Fist looked at me questioningly, and I knew he too would run to join the fray at a nod from me. I stroked the white feather of the fletching and looked to the carnage below. It was all very well to speak coldly of necessary sacrifices while we secured our noose around the enemy, but witnessing the slaughter spreading out below me, all I could think was that these were my people. I hid like a coward in the distance while they were slaughtered to buy us time.

Well, I could buy time too.

I signaled the Fist and together we rose from the grass and charged down the incline, howling to draw the Skeltai's attention. Noticing our arrival, a number of their warriors turned away from the helpless villagers and advanced toward us. I paused at the foot of the hill long enough to fire several arrows into the nearest of them. My Fist companion ran on ahead of me, a battle cry on his lips, sword raised to sweep off the head of the first Skeltai to fall in his path. I had to admire him. Not many men would have the courage to plunge headfirst and alone into an overwhelming sea of enemies, but that was exactly what he did. They swarmed over the lone Fist like starving ants, and the last I saw of him was the flash of his blood-streaked blade, silvery beneath the moonlight, as they closed over him.

They were too close for shooting now, and I had just time enough to replace my bow with a pair of knives before the first of them was upon me. He threatened me with a long spear, and I held up my pitiful knives. I could image only one outcome from this match. I hadn't expected to be caught up in the fighting or I would have armed myself appropriately.

But suddenly more shouts echoed through the night, and I started, nearly making the fatal mistake of looking over my shoulder to see where they came from. Could Captain Delecarte and his men have come to our aid so soon?

The Skeltai I faced took advantage of my hesitation and drove his spear at my side, grazing flesh as I dodged a second too slow to avoid him.

While I staggered to keep my feet under me, dropping one of my knives to clutch my burning side, an arrow whizzed through the air and took my opponent through the throat. Now I dared look back up the hill to see a handful of dark figures barreling down toward the fray. I recognized the bowman by his stance, although it was too dark to see faces over the distance. Rot it all! I had told Dradac to hold the others back! Why did no one listen to my orders unless it pleased him?

But it might be just as well they had showed up. I certainly wasn't making any headway toward a heroic rescue on my own. The first of my men to reach me tossed me his own blade in passing, taking up the spear of the fallen Skeltai, which he then wielded against the coming onslaught with surprising skill. The full wave of Skeltai warriors broke upon us then, and I had my hands full defending myself against their long spears and the light throwing axes they directed with amazing accuracy.

One of those axes spun toward me now. I braced for its impact, but a careless combatant stepped between me and the spinning blade, taking the weapon in the back.

We were vastly outnumbered, each of us fully focused on our own defense to survive one moment to the next. Any thought of aiding the villagers remained only that—a fleeting thought. I was vaguely aware of the carnage still taking place around me, of screaming villagers and cabins now ablaze. But all my attention was on blocking and counterstrokes and adapting to the unbalancing new concept of facing spearmen with a broadsword, something I'd had no training to do.

I was fighting back-to-back with Dradac. Even in the midst of a melee in the dark, there was no mistaking the giant.

"What was the idea?" I gasped breathlessly at him, knocking aside a spear plunging for my midsection. "I thought I told you to hang back in the trees."

"Change of plans," he countered. "You didn't say you were about to go running out and hold back the Skeltai single-handed." He sounded as casual as if we were exchanging information over dinner instead of ringed in on all sides by an overwhelming flood of enemies.

"Doesn't matter what I decide to do." I panted, evading another spear by a hair's breadth and slashing back at the enemy. "I'm the leader. You're supposed to obey me."

No time to look, but I could hear his grin. "I'll apologize after I finish saving your hide."

"*My* hide?"

For response, he launched a one-man assault into the middle of his enemies. They gave way before him, seemingly taken aback at the big man's daring, and he disappeared from view.

Somewhere in the distance, a horn sounded. The trumpeting scarcely penetrated my concentration, and when it did, I first thought it an enemy signal. But then my ears caught the thundering approach of an oncoming arm of cavalry. I risked a fleeting glance at the rise of the hill and caught a glimpse of shadowy horsed figures plunging over the crest and into view.

It was about time the Fists showed up.

The Skeltai warriors were now the ones outnumbered and must have realized it immediately. But they didn't break and run immediately. Evidently determined to salvage what they could of the endeavor, they slowed their retreat enough to snatch up terrified villagers in singles and twos as they ran and drove them ahead of them into the trees.

My first impulse was to run after them, but as the horsemen bore down on us, I was forced to discard the idea and stand aside lest I be trampled by my own soldiers. Somewhere in the flood of cavalrymen streaming by, I caught a glimpse of the Praetor, his red cape billowing out behind him. I also saw Terrac near the head of the line.

After holding to one side to let them pass, I took off on their heels in pursuit of the enemy. I dodged shadowy trees and brambles as they rose before me. The crashing and stamping sounds nearby told me the Fists on horseback were impeded by the density of the forest. They would eventually be forced to dismount and abandon their animals if they hoped to catch the retreating war party.

As I ran, I followed the enemy by sound and sense. It was impossible to see anything of them in the brief flashes of moonlight slanting through the treetops. I stumbled on a fallen branch and caught myself, slumping against a thick tree to catch my breath. The sounds of the fleeing raiders were much closer now, and the main body of our men seemed to have fallen back in the distance, slowed by the burden of their horses and their unfamiliarity with the terrain. I found myself alone and in the lead.

Ahead a patch of starlight filtered through the leafy canopy, illuminating a small clearing. Here I made out a startling sight. Dozens of Skeltai warriors converged on the spot, driving their captives along before them. One by one, each disappeared into a ring of blue fire flaming in the forest floor. I had long known their method of travel but had only seen it in action once before. Amazed, I hung back in the shadows until I watched the last of the Skeltai warriors leap into the burning hole in the earth and disappear from view, carrying the hapless village prisoners with them.

Dradac collided into me, Ada right behind him, and together we approached the fiery ring with caution. The main body of the Praetor's soldiers arrived. There was a general milling and confusion as no one was overeager to be the first to approach the magic portal.

"Captain Delecarte." I heard the Praetor raise his voice above the confusion. "Get your men through that portal before it closes."

No answer followed his order. One of the Fists said, "The captain's not here, my lord. He was unhorsed during the fight."

The Praetor cursed and demanded, "Where's my lieutenant then?"

No one knew.

"Allow me to go, my lord."

As the brave offer fell on my ears, I squeezed my eyes closed. *Not now, priest boy. Make a hero of yourself some other day.*

But of course Terrac couldn't hear my thoughts, and he stepped confidently forward, signaling others to follow. They did so with obvious reluctance until about half our number stood gathered around the edge of the fiery hole, looking down into the darkness on the other side.

I was among them.

Terrac caught my eye and frowned at me for joining him, but he kept silent. I knew he couldn't attempt to dissuade me from coming without injuring the courage of his men.

Below us, I could see sticks and leaves littering a forest floor that looked much like this one. But it was ever darker on that side of the portal than this. I pushed my way to the front of the men ringing the glowing portal and signaled Dradac and the others of my circle back when they would have joined me. I willed them to obey me this once, and for a wonder, they did. I savored that victory, aware it could be my last. If I stepped through that portal, I had no solid expectation of returning to see any of them again.

But I looked at Terrac, apparently fearless, as he prepared to descend through the glowing ring, and I knew I had no choice but to follow him.

Why? The question came in the same breath. The Praetor had given no orders to me. Even the bow remained strangely silent. There was nothing forcing me to join the others on this fatal mission. Nothing save the fact my one-time friend was among those embarking on the suicidal quest. Common sense and every survival instinct I possessed cautioned me to pull out while I still could. But as I watched Terrac step into the portal, his head and shoulders disappearing into the darkness below, I knew I would give in to a pull stronger than either of these.

I was next through the hole.

* * *

I fell a short distance, landing across Terrac's legs, and we scrambled to one side, out of the way of the next fellow leaping down. It was even darker on this side of the portal than it had been in Dimming, and the treetops were so thick and dense overhead they blocked out even the occasional moonbeams that had dotted the canopy in that other forest. I knew it was Terrac who offered a hand to haul me to my feet only by the sense of him and the fact the next men were still scrambling through the portal behind us.

Five. Six. I counted the dark figures dropping down through the window above and lost track of what happened to them after they collapsed together in a confused heap in the darkness. The creak and chink of armor, heavy breathing sounds, and muffled curses as they scrambled to their feet told me they remained nearby. Even these odd sounds were comforting as they were the only assurance I had I wasn't stranded alone in this new world. There was also the solid feel of Terrac beside me. I didn't even pause to consider whether it was his actual physical form I felt or merely the sense of his presence. Either was all the reassurance I needed.

I kept my eyes on the Fists dropping through the hole, and at the count of eleven, I noticed something was wrong. The eerie blue light of the glowing portal was fading. We had only an instant's warning, and then the portal began to warp and shrink even as the feet of the twelfth man appeared in the circle of light above.

"Wait!" I shouted. "The portal's closing!"

Even as I screamed my warning, the window drew in on itself and closed, both the man and his feet disappearing. There was silence in the darkness around us as we all struggled to take in the fact we were now irrevocably trapped this side of the portal with no way to return. And there were only thirteen of us, not the hundred that had been planned.

"W-what do you think happened to Beric?" one of the Fists ventured to ask of the man who hadn't made it through.

I shrugged before remembering no one could see the gesture in the dark.

"I suspect he's had his feet cut off or worse," I said. "We can only guess what happens to anyone who finds himself stuck halfway through the portal."

There was a general murmur of uneasiness at that, and I realized my mistake. To admit none of us knew anything about the operation of the portals was more disturbing than if the danger were a known one. Terrac must have realized it too, because he immediately set about getting their minds fixed on something more familiar.

"All right, soldiers, gather round," he directed, his low voice penetrating the darkness.

The shifting of feet and snapping of twigs underfoot were the only indications his order was being obeyed, but he went on with as much confidence as if he could see us grouping around him. "You all know this wasn't according to plan. There were meant to be more of us down here. A lot more."

Muttered agreement met his words, but he didn't pause to commiserate.

"Now we find ourselves only a dozen in number, trapped miles into enemy territory with no provisions and nothing but the weapons we carry to defend ourselves. There can be no reinforcements—you all understand why—and there will probably be no way out for us when our mission here is complete."

There were unhappy sounds of agreement from the others.

Terrac's tone grew surprisingly sharp. "Well I ask you, so what? Should we sit and cower, waiting for passing savage scouts to find us and put an end to our plight? Or should we act like our lord's men? Maybe passing through magic portals and entering enemy lands wasn't something we expected when we got out of bed this morning…"

There were soft chuckles at that.

"But our orders remain clear, to strike at the enemy where they feel themselves safe, to harass them in whatever possible way. No part of that hinges on our being alive at the end of the day. The important thing is for the Skeltai to know we're capable of striking at their very heart."

There arose a noise of agreement, and I felt renewed purpose spreading through the group. I held my peace, but inwardly I was thinking it would take more than duty and determination to see any of us through this. I remembered with a pang how Dradac had suggested Ada guide our party home at mission's end and how I had just moments ago waved her away from the mouth of the portal when she would have followed me. It was I who had sunk our only hope of returning home. But there seemed no need to give voice to the fact. It was already too late. For now, I had to cast in my lot with a bunch of Fists, something I never thought to do, and hope by some miracle we would come through this.

Terrac was organizing the men now. The first thing we had to do was ascertain where we were and the distance from the nearest Skeltai settlement. Both tasks seemed impossible in this inky blackness. But looking around me, I found my eyes were slowly adjusting to the nighttime world of the Black Forest. I could just make out the looming shapes of trees on all sides. The ground at my feet might as well have been a gaping hole for all I could see of it, but by shuffling my feet carefully, I avoided tripping over rocks and roots.

My companions were going through a similar exploration. I heard thuds and muffled oaths as they stumbled into trees and collided with obstacles on the uneven earth. It seemed to me by the slope of the forest floor that we were on the downside of a gentle hill, but that deduction didn't help us much. Another cracking sound and a loud howl from somewhere to my right brought Terrac's wrath down on the offender.

"Quiet, you imbeciles! Do you want to alert every Skeltai within miles of our presence?"

"No, sir. Sorry, sir."

"I don't want sorry. I want you to use your head. They could be anywhere. For all we know there's an army of them surrounding us even now, laughing as they watch us stumble around like blind men."

This declaration sobered us all, and I heard the whisper of more than one sword being drawn and held ready in case of just such a situation.

We made our way down the hill for what I suspected was no sounder reason than it was easier traveling down than up in the gloom. The nearest Skeltai civilization was as likely to be one direction as another, so we took the way easiest on our feet. There was a lot of grumbling as we walked. It turned out men outfitted in heavy leather and mail weren't very nimble on their feet when stumbling half-blind down a hill. I wasn't alone in losing my balance repeatedly and sliding a good distance before I could get my feet under me again.

The third time this happened I skidded to a halt, rolling into a fallen log, and righted myself just in time to look up into the pale face of a Skeltai warrior.

Chapter Five

I had no time to react or dodge the blow of the blunt-ended weapon that fell across my face in the next second. Pain exploded across my face, and I heard a sickening, crunching sound I recognized as that of my nose breaking. I was vaguely aware of the cries of my companions in the background, but their shouts grew distant as I sank to my knees, fighting to retain consciousness. I swiftly lost the struggle and plunged into a well of darkness.

* * *

When next I awoke, it was to a strange floating sensation and the feeling of all the blood rushing to my head. On second thought, I realized floating was too pleasant a term for it. I was being jounced roughly along with the world around me passing by in a confused, shadowy blur. I made out the shapes of boulders and trees on either side, but they seemed to be standing on their heads. Then I realized it was I and not they who was upside down and being carried slung over someone's shoulder like a sack of potatoes. It took me a moment to figure out how I had come to be in this posture.

The face of the Skeltai looming up at me out of the darkness flashed before my eyes, and I recalled the startled cries of my companions as they too were taken in the surprise attack. Recollection brought a surge of panic. I began wriggling feebly to right myself, but my injury had sapped the strength out of me and I succeeded only in digging my captor's hard shoulder deeper into my belly. The broad arm across the backs of my thighs that held me in my precarious position tightened a little.

"Will you be still?" A low voice whispered from beneath me. "You're only drawing their attention, and I don't think that can be good for either of us."

"Terrac?" I tried to lift my head to get a look at the man who carried me, but the only view I was afforded could have belonged to anybody. I tried to think beyond the weakness in my head and the pounding behind my eyeballs. My face felt numb except for a little trickle of wetness I suspected was blood running from my smashed nose.

I asked, "Are you and the others all right? Are we prisoners or are we escaping?"

"Sshhh…," he hissed sharply. "I'm better off than you are, but we can't talk right now. The savages don't like it. Just hold on and we'll see what happens next."

I attempted to form some response but wasn't sure if anything made it past my lips before the dizziness washed over me again and the darkness rose to drag me down.

* * *

Cool hands moved over me. Terrac's, I thought, comforted. But when I opened my eyes, it was to look into a strange pair of expressionless, dark orbs peering out of a bloodless, white face. I lunged upright, nearly feinting again at the dizziness the motion sent rushing through my head.

A wild look around revealed I was lying in some sort of shadowy, low-roofed hut. The only light was cast from the glow of a dying fire in a bed of stones built up in the center of the hut. This allowed me to see I was surrounded by a circle of savages, half-naked but for the animal hides and feathers they wore like decorations and the blood-red paint swirling in intricate designs over their bodies. The glow of the fading embers cast an eerie orange light across their features, making them look like some nightmarish vision from another world.

At my sudden stirring, some of them jumped back a little. Still others reached for spears or blunt weapons, and there arose an unintelligible muttering among them, though none moved any farther to do me harm. Each had his gaze fixed unwaveringly upon me, and there was no question I had been and still was the object of whatever mysterious gathering was taking place here.

I had no notion as to what they were planning for me or what fate had already befallen my companions. But neither question was my primary concern. My most immediate thought was of my bow and whether it was safe. Instinctively I reached to check it was still in place, discovering as I did so my hands remained unbound. I couldn't imagine why.

The bow was no longer slung across my back.

The disarmament came as no surprise, but that didn't prevent the jolt of helplessness I felt at finding it gone. This must have shown in my eyes because the nearest of my Skeltai captors, an aged man with silvery hair and a face so heavily lined with wrinkles I could scarcely discern the features behind them, leaned forward. There was something familiar about him, but recognition eluded me. It was this man who had been bending over me when I woke. He looked into my eyes intently now and uttered some words I couldn't understand in a voice that was cracked and reedy.

I swallowed my fear and shook my head to show my lack of understanding.

"Barra-banac. *Barra-banac*," he repeated insistently, gesturing to the floor at my side.

Where had I heard that phrase before? Something triggered my memory. It was the Skeltai name for my bow, wasn't it? I followed the old man's gestures and found the bow lying on the dirt floor just a finger's breadth from my hand.

Relief washed over me, and I didn't even attempt to hide my eagerness as I snatched the weapon up in my hands. My arrows were nowhere in sight, but it didn't matter. I felt more confident just for holding it. A ripple of murmurs passed through the other onlooking Skeltai, but the old one regarded me calmly. He made a sharp motion for silence, and I gathered by the way his friends instantly obeyed him that he was a person of importance or authority.

I wondered what it was they wanted with me, why each regarded me with an expression of mingled distrust and distaste yet also with something more in their eyes. A glint of admiration, maybe bordering on respect. This made no sense. I drew in a breath and became aware of a tightness around my ribs.

Looking down, I found a scrap of clean woven cloth wrapped tightly around my upper torso, spots of dried blood showing through. I had all but forgotten the graze I had taken during my earlier brush with the Skeltai war party back in Dimmingwood. Even the more recent blow I'd taken across the cheek and nose now seemed an eternity ago. Had my savage captors been the ones responsible for bandaging the wound? Something in the old one's face told me it was so. I realized for the first time the sticky blood had also been wiped away from my nose and upper lip where I had taken the more recent blow across my face. Something was strange in all this.

But before I could put any more thought to it, I was startled out of my confusion by a series of defiant shouts and strangled curses filtering in from outside. My heart leapt into my throat. *Terrac.*

"Rot the lot of you! What are they doing to her?" he was shouting. "A plague take you all! If you've hurt her, I'll slaughter every one of you filthy, corpse-skinned…"

The old Skeltai before me made an impatient chopping motion with his hand, and the tent immediately emptied as his followers dashed to do his bidding.

"What a minute," I cried, leaping to my feet. "Where are they going?"

I was blocked from following them by a pair of remaining savages who seized hold of my arms and deposited me, not roughly but firmly, back on the floor with the old one. Outside the sounds of a brief struggle ensued, and then Terrac's shouts cut off abruptly.

"What happened out there?" I demanded of the old Skeltai. "What did you tell your leeches to do to my friend?"

I dove for the old man, but the two savages were upon me again, and this time they didn't release their hold until my hands were bound firmly behind my back.

An accented voice emerged from the shadows. "Forgive our crudeness. We wish to treat you with the respect the holder of the barra-banac deserves, but your... anger makes this difficult."

I turned toward the voice.

I had counted only four savages remaining in the tent, but here was one whose presence had somehow escaped me. I started as the glow of the dying fire fell across his strong, youthful features, highlighting the blue streaks in his hair and the gracefully decorative scars etched across his torso. I knew this man. It took me a moment to place where I had seen him before, and then I remembered. The last time we had met had been inside a crumbling hut in the middle of Dimmingwood. He had been bruised and bloodied, beaten into silence but never submission, by those under my command. Only then a length of rope and a half dozen of my friends with sharp weapons had stood between us. That was no longer the case.

He smiled, saying, "You recognize me. This is good."

He gestured toward the old man. "My grandfather understands that you and I are old friends, and he has been good enough to give us this chance to face one another again."

The old man who appeared to be the leader here was his grandfather? In my worst dreams I had never imagined I would again face the Skeltai scout I had once tortured or that he might ever have the opportunity to even the score. My belly lurched as I wondered what cruel tricks these pale-skinned blood seekers were capable of devising to raise a prisoner's screams. They probably knew methods of torture our more civilized society couldn't even imagine. No wonder they hadn't wanted me to die too quickly of my wounds.

Crazed laughter tried to work its way up my throat, and I had to clamp my jaws down to hold it in. It was no good going out of my mind before they had even touched me.

Some hint of that laughter must have touched my face because the Skeltai scout said, "Something amuses you?"

"Only my situation," I said. "I hadn't thought to lay eyes on you again, savage, and yet fate has laid me at your very doorstep. And this time I am the one bound and helpless." I hesitated at the memory, admitting, "Perhaps I deserve that. I don't know."

He chose his words carefully, and the way he continually paused, searching for the right one, showed me his grasp of my tongue, though very good, knew its limits. "The path of fate twists in circles no mortal can foresee," he admitted. "But I do not share your surprise for I have always known we were destined to meet again. For many days and nights I dreamed only of exacting my revenge for the time you held me captive. You did not know it, but you stretched the limits of my endurance. You almost made me betray my people, and for that shameful lapse of strength I could not forgive you. I need not forgive you still. For my grandfather has made me see the ultimate vengeance lies not in breaking you as you would have broken me but in striving toward the greater goal of my people. When we destroy this province of yours, that will be our ultimate victory. What are petty squabbles beside this final glory?"

He seemed to be taking a lot for granted, and I wondered what gave him such confidence. That his uncivilized tribes could fully conquer my province with its modern weaponry and well-trained fighting men was uncertain. But I wasn't about to spark a debate on the subject.

Instead I said, "I'm a little confused about where this is headed. Pardon me if I cut straight to the point. What happens to me now? Am I going to die?"

He shrugged. "That is up to you, young kinswoman."

"Kinswoman? Why do you call me that?" I asked, startled.

He tilted his head and examined me. "You haven't the sun-darkened skin and dark hair of our enemies. You are of our Skeltai ancestry, are you not?"

I scowled. "You're mistaken. We may share common ancestors, but my kinsmen stayed in the province and became civilized long ago."

He raised blue-streaked eyebrows. "Such contempt for your rightful people."

I knew what he was doing. "Stop pretending your people are mine," I said. "I have no patience for your foreign tricks."

"One in your position has cause to cultivate infinite patience," he pointed out. "But I see you think of nothing at this moment but your fate. So let me explain how you find yourself here. Our plan was to lure your soldiers through the portal where you would make prime sacrifices for tonight's Sagara Nouri ritual. Understand, stupid villagers are acceptable sacrifices and vast numbers of them, harvested from your province, will be committed to the fires. But when possible, something more... special is preferred. Good fighting men, strong warriors who go to their deaths with brave hearts, are the sacrifices we value most."

With each word my heart sank deeper, every new detail like another pebble added to the weight of the burden crushing down on me. How easily we had been duped! And it was my fault. I should have quashed the idea of trapping the Skeltai before it had even formed itself into a full plan. I should have seen our enemies were too clever to allow themselves to be tricked so easily.

The old man, the one Blue Hair called his grandfather, was jabbering at me in his outlandish tongue again. He reached out a wrinkled white hand to touch the bow where it had fallen at my feet.

I scowled, asking, "Does he have to be here?"

"You should be grateful he is. Without his in-inter…?"

"Intervention," I supplied.

"Yes. Without that, you would be dead now. Injured as you were, it would have been easier for the war party to dispose of you than bring you back with the others. But my grandfather is a great shaman, and upon seeing in a vision that you would soon enter our forest, he commanded you should live."

I abruptly realized where I'd seen the old shaman before. It had been after the attack on Boulder's Cradle. Dradac, Ada, and I had pursued the fleeing Skeltai and arrived in time to see them disappearing into one of their portals. When I looked through after them, I'd seen this wizened, silver-haired old man's bloodless face looking back at me.

I remembered now how that look had inspired me with a fear that returned to haunt me on many sleepless nights. It was he who had activated the portal, he who had somehow foreseen my coming and had made certain I would arrive in this place to find myself as I was now—a prisoner at his feet. I could only guess how much of the attack on Beaver Creek, our wild scheme to trap the Skeltai, and our disastrous pursuit through the portal had all been a part of his greater scheme.

I looked into his small, dark eyes, and he returned my gaze with a knowingness that sent a shudder down my spine. I could have sworn he was reading my mind. Impossible. But I found I couldn't meet the shaman's eyes. If I did, he might see through my calm façade, might see the fear coursing through me as I contemplated his power and tried to guess its limits.

"What does this mean, the way he keeps touching my bow?" I hadn't realized I was about to speak until the words had already drawn themselves from my mouth.

The Sageuon muttered some words to his grandson in their barbaric tongue, and through the younger Skeltai the meaning was interpreted.

"He says there is a legend of a Skeltai warrior, one who was great among our people long ago, before the strangers came and claimed the land across the border. Because of his enchanted bow, we called him the barra-banac or Bearer of the Bow. When he died, the magical bow was lost to us, but prophecy told of how it would be rediscovered and of the one who would one day hold it again. A new Bearer of the Bow. My grandfather wishes to be that bearer."

"That will not happen," I said fiercely without stopping to think. "The bow is mine, and while I live, no other will hold it." They didn't like that much. I could tell by their expressions as they conferred in low voices.

The bow grew warm, but I couldn't focus on its anger. I was too filled with my own. Or were the two one and the same? It was difficult to tell anymore.

The younger Skeltai pulled back from the elder and returned his attention to me.

"The barra-banac is not a plaything for a youngling. Its magic is great and ancient, a power you are scarcely capable of comprehending. With it, our people could do great things, could accomplish victories you cannot imagine. It belongs with us."

Glaring, I said, "The bow has chosen its bearer, and I won't give it up. If you want to kill me and take it, I can't stop you. But I warn you I'll bloody well try."

The blue-haired Skeltai scowled while relaying my message to his grandfather, and when he interpreted the old man's response, I could tell he didn't like what he was compelled to admit.

"We cannot take the bow from its holder by force. As long as it recognizes you as its true possessor, in all other hands it would be only a lifeless piece of wood and string. You must give us the bow willingly."

I snorted, anger making me bold. "You're wasting your time."

The young savage snapped. "Do not be foolish! We hold your life and the lives of your friends in the palms of our hands. You would be wise to strike a bargain with us. The shaman is prepared to make a generous offer. Your freedom if you gift us the bow."

I smirked. "I refuse the offer."

The Skeltai thrust his face close to mine, the dangerous glint of his eyes reminding me how much animosity he felt against me, however restrained he had appeared to this point.

"Ignorant dog!" he growled. "You have no idea of the shaman's condescension in bargaining with you. On no other occasion would my grandfather look a half-blood in the eye, but today he deals with you as with an equal, as with one of our people."

"Does he always keep equals bound in his presence?" I couldn't resist asking.

"It is his wisdom to do as he pleases!" was the retort. "You should not be in his presence at all. You walk beneath the sun, not in the cool shadows of the deep forest. You live within walls of stone, not sleeping beneath the roof of the trees."

"I've actually spent many a night sprawled in the branches of a tree," I said truthfully. "You savages aren't the only ones with forests."

He scoffed. "Your forests are dead wood and half-grown saplings. You of the provinces do not know deep shadow."

He made it sound as if this were a terrible shame on us.

The old shaman interrupted our argument to speak a few words. Although I understood none of the exchange between them, I sensed the younger man was being rebuked.

After a pause, the chastened young Skeltai grumbled, "My grandfather wishes to return the talk to our bargain."

I leaned forward. "You have already told me if the bow were yours you would use it as a powerful weapon against my province. How then can you expect me to willingly give it up to you? No, I'll never do that. Tell the old man if he's interested in making any other kind of bargain, I'm willing to talk. I'll trade him almost anything he wishes to buy the freedom of my companions. But the bow I will not give up."

Cannot give up, I amended inwardly. I doubted I could separate myself from the bow if I tried. But there was no reason for my enemies to know this.

Shooting me a scorching look, my interpreter passed on this information to the shaman.

The old man turned cold eyes on me, and my resolve almost weakened with sudden fear. When he spoke his voice was like a dash of ice water.

"My grandfather says," I was told, "that he has no other bargain for you. If you will not pass the bow into our hands, we will offer both you and it as a gift to our gods. Maybe such a large sacrifice will incline the gods to our favor, and they will see fit to give us victory over our enemies without the barra-banac."

I could tell by the wild expression of the old shaman he was mad enough to carry out his threat. But even now I didn't consider complying with their wishes. What I needed, I thought frantically, was to buy myself more time. Time for escape, for rescue. Time for a miracle…

I said, "We can play at this game all night, but you'll not change my mind."

"Then you will burn on the fires of Sagara Nouri, and the corpses of your friends will be the kindling at your feet."

There wasn't much I could say to that, but I clung to the shreds of my determination and wouldn't allow myself to contemplate the picture he painted.

My captors conferred together, and when my interpreter turned back to me, he said, "It has been decided you will be given the opportunity to consider the shaman's offer and to imagine the fate you will suffer if you refuse it. But your time must be short for the rites begin at the midpoint of the night."

He called in the pair of savages lurking in the background, and I was hauled unceremoniously from the hut and out into the black of the night.

Chapter Six

In the surrounding darkness, I had only a brief impression of thick, shadowy trees reaching out to clutch at me with their sharp branches as I was maneuvered down a beaten path away from the little hut. It was difficult to make out my surroundings in much detail. The dense canopy overhead blotted out all but the most determined slivers of moonlight, so it was as if I stumbled around in a dark closet with only the aid of my captors to keep my feet on the path.

When we came into a narrow clearing, I could identify a little more of what was before me because of a faint orangey glow flickering through the dense foliage in the distance. I couldn't see what lay in the larger clearing beyond this and wondered if the firelight I was glimpsing through the trees was from the same fires meant to consume my body and those of my companions during the coming blood rites.

I pushed the thought from my mind. Escape was what I had to concentrate on, not the consequences if I failed to achieve that goal. I looked around and noted the area was ringed with rows of large cages that looked much like outdoor prison cells constructed of wooden bars.

I was hauled to the nearest of these and made to stand waiting in the care of one of my guards as the other deftly unlatched and opened the door. Should I break free and run? But no, the savage's hold on me was firm. Besides, my hands remained bound. The opportunity passed as I was seized and hurled roughly into the interior.

Driven by the force of my captor's shoves, I stumbled into the far wall. Before I had time to regain my balance and turn, I heard the door behind me being drawn closed and secured. Clutching the narrow wooden bars, I closed my eyes for a second. What cruel twist of fate had brought me into this mess? I had come hunting Skeltai and instead had become their captive. Thinking to damage my enemies, I had stumbled unwittingly into their waiting hands. Not only that, but I'd delivered more victims into their grasp.

I realized I wasn't alone. Looking around me, I identified other sorry figures slumped in dejected poses along the walls of the cage—my companions in this failed venture. Or as many, I supposed, as remained of them. Bloodied and disarmed, the Fists didn't look quite as impressive as they had at the start of the day. Only one of them, a wiry little man I vaguely remembered seeing before, left the shadows to wordlessly help me loosen my bonds before he drifted away.

The moment my hands were free I grabbed my bow, which my captors had slung crookedly and somewhat ridiculously around my neck before bringing me out here. Resettling it in its rightful place across my back, I wondered what had prompted them to let me keep it. I could only guess it had something to do with their grudging reluctance to separate the bow from my hands by force.

Now it was time to assess my chances of escaping this wooden box.

I noticed my fellow prisoners had managed to free themselves of their bonds. But it looked like they had given up after that, and they sat silent and apparently resigned to their fates. Fear was palpable in the air as I did a quick mental count.

Terrac's voice came from a shadowed corner. "Seven of us remain."

Relief flooded through me that he was one of the seven.

He continued with, "The others were killed in the fighting. It might be best if we had shared in their luck, but I'm afraid a slower and more painful road lies ahead for us."

His voice was weak, and I detected a tremor of pain as I scrambled to his sprawled form.

"Terrac, are you all right?" I could see no injuries on him, and it was impossible to tell if the blood spattered across his clothing was his or someone else's. I made a grab for the buckles of his breast plate, but he stopped me.

"Don't look, Ilan. It's too late now."

"I have training," I offered feebly, knowing full well the handful of tricks I had learned at the elbow of Javen the healer weren't enough to save a man with a mortal injury.

He caught my hand at the buckles again.

"Let it be, Ilan," he said.

My eyes stung at the gasp of pain it cost him to get out the words. This was all happening too fast. My world was crashing down around me, and I couldn't take it all in. Life without Terrac would be… no life at all. Funny that revelation came to me at a time like this.

He still held my hand and seemed to be unaware of doing so as he said, "There's a favor I need to ask of you."

I didn't hesitate. "Of course. Anything."

"I need…" He winced, stiffening with pain. "I need you to forgive me."

What was he talking about? I said, "I don't understand. Forgive you for what?"

"Listen. I was wrong to act as I did when you came to rescue me all those years ago in Selbius. I've regretted my words ever since. I've messed up a lot of things. Maybe we both have. I just want everything as it should be now… at the end. I need you forgive me and say we're friends again."

"Of course, of course. We were never anything else."

"You swear to that?"

"I swear it."

He smiled weakly, and I squeezed his hand. Did his life force feel weaker than it had? Did I sense him slipping away even now?

He moved abruptly to hoist himself into a sitting position.

"What are you doing?" I pressed a firm hand on his shoulder. "You should be lying down. Movement will open the wound farther."

He brushed my hand away. "Don't worry about that. I've never felt better."

His weakness fell away like an old cloak, and he was suddenly moving and speaking with the ease of a healthy man.

I looked for a grimace of pain or an outpouring of blood, but there was none.

Satisfied he was uninjured, I shoved him back against the prison bars. But not very hard. I remembered too well the heartrending ache when I'd thought he was dying.

"What's wrong with you, priest boy?" I demanded, reverting in my anger to his childhood nickname. "Who plays such a stupid joke at a time like this?"

"I wasn't joking," he protested. "There were things I needed to say and, oddly enough, it's a lot easier to speak your mind when you're dying."

I hesitated. "Well, are you dying or aren't you?"

"I'm not, but I knew you couldn't refuse me if you thought I was."

I exploded. "*Refuse* you? Why, you sneaking, devious—! How dare you pretend you're—when you're really—?"

Choking on my indignation, I had to stop. It was all I could do not to give him another good slam against the bars.

He grinned. "Now, now. Don't forget you gave your word."

"I promised to forgive everything that happened before," I snapped. "But I won't be tricked into forgetting *this* so easily."

He looked away from me, out the bars of the cage and into the night. I followed his direction and saw the bonfires of the Skeltai in the distance.

"Sadly, I don't think you'll have a very long time to hold the grudge," Terrac said. "They're preparing for our deaths even now."

I sobered. The orangey glow of the bonfires cast a flickering light over us, and the bars of the cage threw long shadows across Terrac's face. His mouth quirked in an apologetic smile, and his violet eyes gleamed beautifully in the half light. It occurred to me suddenly that a man could be forgiven many things when he looked this good.

The moment was interrupted by a piercing howl in the distance as the Skeltai shamans took up a flesh-crawling chant. I shivered at the reminder of our eminent fate, even as I tried to find in myself some spark of hope or defiance.

"We should check the entrance," I suggested.

"Locked and guarded," said Terrac.

"Maybe there's another way out?"

"I already checked."

He startled me by reaching up to run one gloved finger down the bridge of my nose following the crooked spot where it had been freshly broken. A shiver ran through me at the contact.

"It's fine," I said, abruptly pushing his hand away. "It doesn't hurt anymore."

I dabbed self-consciously at the dried blood crusting my upper lip.

"It shouldn't be fine," he said quietly. "You took a hard blow."

I had no desire to explain how the Skeltai shaman had tended my injuries or to relate his offer regarding the bow. Suppose Terrac tried to persuade me to accept the offer and spare all our lives? What I had to do was hard enough. I didn't know if I could hold out against any more pressure.

Unaware of my thoughts, he took hold of my jaw and turned my head from side to side, studying what must have been a fairly impressive bruise spreading from nose to cheek. His hands were gentle.

I swallowed. "I said I'm all right. Could you not do that please?"

I moved to pull away and was surprised when he didn't let me go. My eyes went to his.

I heard a soft snicker from one of the Fists in the background. I had all but forgotten their presence. My cheeks burned, but I supposed it was good that the men could still laugh at something. It showed they hadn't given up altogether.

Terrac snapped at the offender, "Could we have a little privacy please?"

The Fist looked abashed, but one of his companions chipped in cheekily, "We'd be glad to grant you some alone time, sir, but unfortunately the savages have locked us in."

"Then let's be looking for a way out," I said and scrambled to my feet, trying to dust away the foolish feeling that had overtaken me.

I tugged at the bars along the wall, feeling for a loose one. The whole of our party stirred at this faint show of hope and followed my lead, searching for a weak point or another way out. Terrac worked alongside me, and for the first time I was glad of the shadows, knowing they concealed the high color in my cheeks.

We all worked in silence except for the scuffing sounds of feet across the dirt floor and occasional grunts of discouragement when an idea was tested and proved fruitless. I was painfully aware of the time slipping by. Through the bars I could make out the shadowy figures of our savage guards standing by, and although it was too dark to make out their faces over the distance, their heads often turned in our direction. It seemed to me they observed our failed efforts with amusement.

I slowly realized we were wasting our last hours on a doomed attempt. If there was a way to get us out of these cages, away from the Skeltai forest and back home, this wasn't it. I said nothing to the others but let them hold out hope while they could. I stumbled wearily into that same dark corner Terrac and I had shared earlier and sank to the floor, my face resting on my clenched hands. I needed to think. Two possibilities kept repeating themselves in my mind.

One, was it time to reconsider my answer to the shaman? Should I give up the bow? The other question… I pushed it to the back of my mind, doubting I was even capable of carrying out such a feat. Despite Hadrian's tutoring, there was too much about my magic I didn't understand. I could only guess at the risks of what I contemplated being attempted by a novice. But the shaman's offer: our freedom for the bow. It seemed foolish not to trade a simple object of wood and string for my life. Had it been my decision to refuse or was it the bow refusing to release me? I wanted to believe the choice was mine. But in my heart that claim rung hollow. This was about my mind having become so deeply ensnared by the enchantment of the weapon I could no longer call my will my own.

Terrac came to join me. I was very aware of him sitting close beside me, his shoulder touching mine, his knee against my knee. Soothing warmth flooded me, and I couldn't tell if the sensation was only physical or the result of his comforting presence washing over me.

I cleared my throat and said, "I need your advice."

"Really? Since when do you seek my counsel?" he teased gently.

"Since I can't trust my own. A decision needs to be made, and there's something holding me back. I can't be sure of myself."

It was difficult to admit that, even to him. *Especially* to him.

"I'm listening," he said.

"It's about my bow. It's enchanted."

He was silent a moment but looked unsurprised. "I've noted the changes in you since you took up that weapon," he admitted. "But I said nothing because my suspicions seemed foolish."

"Don't be so quick to doubt your instincts," I answered. "This bow holds a life and a magic all its own. I've carried it with me long enough to know. It slips into your mind, guiding thoughts and decisions until you can no longer be sure where you end and it begins."

And then I told him. I opened the gates and poured out everything from the night I found the bow right up to this one, admitting all the strange choices I had made, the brave decisions that had been so unlike me. I confessed my doubts as to whether it had been the real Ilan at all who had been responsible for her actions of late. I'd never shared these thoughts with another person. I had been alone inside myself with only the bow for company for too long. Sharing felt good, and yet even as I did it, a tiny voice inside my head whispered recriminations.

Traitor! Betrayer of secrets! We do not need this man who fights with the long steel claw. He is a threat to us!

I gritted my teeth.

Get out of my mind! I want to make my own choices again, to trust my instincts without questioning where they come from!

Terrac must have guessed at the storm raging in my head.

"Maybe you should give me the bow," he said gently. "I'll toss it through the bars, far into the night, and you'll be free of it."

I flinched and grabbed the bow as if to protect it, even though he made no move to act on his suggestion. He waited patiently for me to ask. But I could not.

"There are consequences to be considered," I said, stalling.

"What consequences? Surely we are to die soon enough anyway," he said.

"That's just it. The bow could be the key to our freedom. All I have to do is say yes."

"What do you mean?"

I told him all the Skeltai had revealed to me of the bow and of their great desire to possess it. I left nothing out—not the threats against the province or my loathing of their offer.

When I finished, his expression was thoughtful.

"So this holds the key to all our lives," he said.

He reached out to touch the bow, and I had to steel myself against stopping him. Even now it was hard to see another handling the thing I was so possessive of.

"This decision must be yours," he told me.

"I have made it already."

"And you decided not to give the bow up?"

My gut twisted with guilt.

Yes. I will sacrifice all our lives to keep the thing.

But I couldn't stop the words that came out. "There is nothing else for me to do," I said. "I think giving the bow up would destroy me more thoroughly than anything the Skeltai could do."

"Then you must keep it."

"What? How can you say that?" I asked. "By trading this bow, I could save us."

"This isn't about saving us. It's about saving our homes and our province. Didn't the Skeltai tell you that's why they wanted the bow, to destroy us? What good would it do any of us to get home again only to watch our land crumble, destroyed by the very weapon we placed in our enemy's hands? What would be worth such a tragedy?"

I looked at him. "You've changed so much. Every time I think I've got to a place where I understand you again, you throw me another surprise. The Terrac I remember would trade his own mother to buy life. Now I'm offering you a chance to trade something else, a possession that isn't even yours, to avoid a gruesome death, and you refuse."

"You've changed too over the last couple of years. But not all changes are bad."

As he spoke I felt his gauntleted hand creep over mine. I resisted the startled instinct to snatch my hand away and sat still until the hammering of my heart slowed. Gradually I began to feel comfortable with his hand resting atop mine, and the silence lost its awkwardness. For a brief while I could almost forget our impending doom.

Nighttime insects buzzed around us, and a sharp rock jutted from the earth beneath me, but I was reluctant to slap at the bugs or to shift and resettle myself. If either of us moved or spoke, the gentle spell would be broken and whatever was passing between us in the stillness would be lost.

It was Terrac who broke the silence. "Ilan, if death is around the corner, there's something I'd like to get off my conscience before I go. Call it the old priest boy in me."

Now he had me curious. "All right. What is it?" I asked.

"Remember the last day we were together in Dimmingwood? Back in Red Rock cave, when neither of us realized the Fists were surrounding us?"

I remembered all too well. It had been the first time the bow made me aware of its influence.

He went on. "You and I argued over a leather packet you kept hidden in the wall. You wouldn't tell me your secret plans or let me see what was in the parcel. I guess that made me angry. So on our way outside I pretended to fall against you, using the opportunity to steal your packet and slip it into my jerkin."

I thought of the parcel and the brooch from my mother that had been nestled inside.

I said, "I searched my clothes for that packet later. It was something very precious to me. Not until much later did I realize you had taken it."

"I'm truly sorry. But it didn't matter in the end because I didn't get the chance to open the thing. We were ambushed by the Fists, and I was carried away prisoner. I woke in the dungeon of the Praetor's keep with him standing over me, demanding to know where I had come by the brooch inside that packet. He claimed it belonged to his family and asked if my father had given it to me. I was in so much pain at the time. I didn't understand what was happening. So I gave the answer he seemed to want—a lie. I said yes, the brooch was my father's, given to me on his deathbed. After that he healed me. He returned the brooch to me—told me to wear it proudly. We never spoke of it again, but it was immediately after this that he made a place for me in his household."

My pulse pounded in my head. All the pieces of the puzzle were suddenly falling into place. So much about Terrac's connection to the Praetor now made sense. Only none of it was really about Terrac at all. It was about me.

I seemed to hear my mama's voice echoing back from the past. A snatch of overheard conversation between her and Da.

"But your family..."

"Are far away, and they don't know we have a child. Even if they did, what does it matter? I'm sure his anger has cooled by now—"

For the first time, I knew who *he* was. I remembered the miniature portrait of my father hidden inside the Praetor's silver box. Remembered how my parents had feared the fury of a dangerous relative who forbade them to be together out of hatred for mama's magic.

I began to tremble and felt sweat break out on my face.

"Ilan? Are you all right?" Terrac asked with concern.

I waved him to silence. He was suddenly the last person I wanted to discuss this with, considering how much his theft of the brooch had unsettled both our lives. I scowled fiercely at my feet and turned the truth over in my mind, trying to get used to it.

In the background the chanting of the savages grew louder and faster, as if they built toward the central point of their ceremony.

I tried to set aside Terrac's revelation and think of a solution to our immediate danger. Closing my eyes, I breathed deeply, counting my heartbeats and turning my thoughts inward. The singing of the Skeltai faded until there was only me alone in the darkness, me—and the bow's subtle yet familiar presence vaguely tickling at the back of my mind.

I centered my thoughts on stillness, on peace, and stretched toward the well of magic always just a short distance away. There must be no hurry here. I had all the time in the world.

There it was. A deep, cool pool at the edge of my vision. I had no idea what the magic actually looked like, but it always helped if I mentally summoned this image of a well. I envisioned my hand dipping deep into the shadowy pool, setting ripples flowing as I broke the surface. Power rushed through me, thrilling and seductive, but I clung to my purpose. I mustn't be distracted by the endless possibilities the magic offered. I had come for one thing only.

I drew deeply on the magic, then holding the power wrapped within me, I released the image of the well and slipped back into darkness. This was the tricky part. I had no idea how the Skeltai shaman did it, so I had to explore the shadows blindly, searching for the way.

Scouring my mind of doubt, I coaxed the magic.

I needed a window. A small portal, just big enough to let a sliver of light pierce the darkness. Only enough to see the way to my home on the other side.

I envisioned a spot I knew well—a grassy patch at the foot of Horse Head Rock in Dimmingwood. I imagined a tear in the ground, a little black hole ringed with blue fire, a door from this place to that. My manipulation of the magic was clumsy and unpracticed, like trying to paint a picture of a place I had never seen. Except that I had seen the boulder at Horse Head countless times. I knew precisely where the portal must be, visualized the dew-moistened earth where the hole should open, the arrangement of every scattered stick and pebble. I sharpened the image, adding details by the second, sensing clarity to be essential to my task.

Then I created the portal.

I held my breath, but nothing happened. There was a narrow circular gash in the earth below the Horse Head boulder, but there was no fiery blue ring. Just a shallow pit leading to nowhere.

Of course.

I needed to open a window on this side too. I concentrated on the firm earth beneath me, the tiny pebbles poking into my flesh, the uneven slope of the ground. I willed the earth to fall away, dropping me into a dark tunnel…

But no. Nothing was happening on this end. I must be doing something wrong. Already my power felt drained, but I forced myself to redo the mental process, differently this time. Time crawled by. I didn't know how long I struggled to find a solution. I cut rents in the ground all around Horse Head and attempted to open air portals on both this side and that. All I accomplished was slashing and churning the earth in Dimmingwood.

Once or twice in our confining cage a faint breeze stirred the air around me, but I couldn't be sure whether it was due to any efforts of mine. All I could be certain of was that no portal stood open before me.

At last I let go of the magic, surrendering. I couldn't make a portal. Why had I thought I could?

I was exhausted by the effort. My body ached, cramped from sitting motionless for so long, and drops of sweat trickled down my forehead.

"Are you all right?" Terrac asked. "You've been quiet so long I thought you fell asleep sitting up."

I could tell he was impressed I was able to do that in the middle of the horrible situation we were in, so I allowed him to think it. I had never explained to him about my Natural magic, and considering his allegiance to the Praetor, it seemed unwise to do so now.

In the distance the Skeltai chanting rose to a crescendo before abruptly cutting off into silence.

Chapter Seven

The sudden stillness was thick on the air. A night bird screeched in the distance. My breathing and that of the companions around me seemed loud in the darkness. The quiet lasted only a few heartbeats and then was split by a series of terrified screams nearby.

We all scrambled to see what was happening. I put my face to the bars, Terrac following my example, and together we watched the scene unfolding in the clearing. Dark figures in feathers and hides moved among the cages, spears held aloft, the distant glow of the fires revealing splashes of scarlet paint standing out on their pale flesh. The result was hideous, the feathers and animal skins giving the impression of giant beasts walking upright, while the red paint looked like smears of blood.

They flung open doors of cages I hadn't realized were occupied and dragged out terrified men, women, and children, who wailed and wept and tried to plunge away from them. These prisoners were from my province. I recognized the homespun clothing of woodsfolk and the flashes of sun-darkened skin that stood out against the pale flesh of our Skeltai captors.

The savages' spears flashed out to lodge into any who tried to escape the lines they were being shepherded into. It was obvious the captives lacked the strength or courage to save themselves, and they quickly fell into order. Skeltai warriors moved down their ranks with grim efficiency, mercilessly silencing protesters and cutting loose those they killed from the ropes binding them to their partners.

A numbed silence descended, broken only by the guttural grunts of the savages giving one another orders. The lines began to move out of the clearing, toward the firelight glowing through the trees. I knew these kidnapped woodsfolk went to a horrible fate, one I was powerless to prevent.

As if reading my thoughts, Terrac squeezed my hand. "Reconsidering trading the bow?" he whispered.

I licked my lips. "Maybe."

"You told me once you'd die before you'd be parted from it."

"That was before I dreamed anybody would take me up on it."

There was no time to say more. The door of our cage was thrown open, and several dark figures plunged into our midst, hefting threatening spears and herding us away from the walls and toward the door. During the jostling, Terrac's hand slipped from mine and I let it go.

We were shoved roughly into a double line and quickly re-bound, tied wrist to wrist and ankle to ankle with one another, each pair secured by a longer stretch of rope to the one behind it. There was just enough rope to allow walking, but none of us would be able to break into a run without tripping the others or dragging them along. It reminded me of a silly race I used to see children playing in the woods villages. I'd laughed with them then, but it was far less amusing now.

Our captors never turned their eyes from us until we were all secured in this fashion. Then we filed out the door and into the open.

Terrac headed our group in the first row, and I managed to place myself beside him. Despite the calm I tried to project, I was as frightened as anyone, and it was reassuring to be near him. The ropes binding my hand to his were so tight they bit into my skin, but I scarcely minded that. His presence was familiar and comforting. More, it brought out the competitive streak still strong between us, helping me put a brave face on my feelings and wrestle the encroaching panic into submission.

Escape. I had to focus on that hope. I looked at Terrac's face, strong in the glow of the distant fires, and when he caught me watching him, he offered a faint, encouraging smile. He wasn't afraid. So I wouldn't be either.

But it was frustrating to be free of our cage yet prevented from running by both the cord binding us together and the vigilance of our enemies.

Our line attached itself to the end of similar rows of prisoners moving out of the clearing. We followed a lightly beaten path leading a short distance through the trees and into another larger area where the bonfires were located. As our destination came into sight, a commotion broke out ahead. Some of the prisoners, possibly sensing the approach of a horrible fate, even if they didn't know what it was, broke into a frenzy. The line shifted and churned, and the rest of us, being bound together, were pulled into the confusion. Suddenly we were all stumbling into one another's backs, tripping over our ropes.

The Skeltai guards were swift to restore order, their spears darting into the crowd to punish instigators. Cries sounded from the prisoners. The man before me was downed by a spear. In the same instant Terrac dropped limply to the ground. I hadn't seen any blow fall on him. No one had touched him, yet he had collapsed. And now his dead weight dragged at my wrist, forcing me to fall to one knee and crouch over him.

"Terrac? Terrac!" I cried, my voice going high as I used my free hand to shake his shoulder.

There was no response. I bit my lip with no idea if he was truly hurt or if this was some ploy. If it was a game he was playing at, it was a dangerous one.

The Skeltai moved through the disordered crowd, arranging us into lines again. The commotion quickly calmed as the responsible parties were dispatched. Our captors commenced cutting away the handful of dead from our rope lines so we could move forward again. When a pair of savages reached us, they muttered to one another, the larger of the two nudging Terrac with his foot.

My friend didn't move or show any sign of feeling, appearing every bit as dead as the others. I held my breath, praying it truly was only a trick—one he wouldn't be caught in.

The larger Skeltai laughed and said something unintelligible to his companion. Then he was kneeling to cut my wrist free of Terrac's and to sever the ropes joining our ankles. I was hauled to my feet and shoved roughly so that I stumbled forward. The Fists bound behind me had no choice but to follow.

We left Terrac behind, lying motionless on the ground. I didn't dare take even a backward look at him for fear of calling attention. But there was nothing to prevent me stretching out my magic after him, straining to sense his life force. I breathed a sigh of relief when I felt it still burning steadily within him.

I wasn't bitter at his abandoning the rest of us. At this point it was each of us for himself. I only hoped he succeeded at whatever escape he had in mind, even as I stumbled forward to face my own fate.

We passed through the screen of trees and entered a larger clearing ringed by torches and alight in the hotter glow of the bonfires. Bodies filled the space—men, women, and children of all ages, easily identifiable as Skeltai by their bloodless coloring and scanty clothing of animal hides.

They congregated with unnatural stillness and silence for such a great audience, their cold eyes turned on our party as we were led into their presence. This was clearly a solemn occasion for the crowd, their grave attitude doubtless a sign of respect for their shaman and their gods rather than we who were about to lose our lives.

I ignored the strange, unreadable faces turned my way and focused on finding a possible exit from this place if the opportunity came. I looked for a thin point in the crowd, an opening through the mass of bodies ringing us. But there was none.

Fighting down despair, I tried to think instead of Terrac running free somewhere out there. At least one of us had escaped this horror. Would he ever find his way home, or was he doomed to be picked up by the enemy?

As we prisoners were forced through the path opened by the crowd, the heat of the bonfires drove away the chill of the night. The skins of my fellow captives and those of our silent observers gleamed with sweat beneath the eerie torchlight, and I imagined mine did too. The roaring fires were built on piles of dried logs, their flames reaching so high if there had been any overhanging branches from the forest trees they would have caught fire. Cinders and black smoke swirled on a draft that carried them up into the night sky.

It was a long time since there had been a break in the overhead canopy to allow me a glimpse of the stars. Now I took comfort in the familiarity of the starlight and my brief glimpse of the moon as it slid behind a silvery cloud.

As long as I kept my eyes fixed on the skies, I could forget how I had fallen into this new world of nightmares and shadows.

We were led in a double line through our audience. Their faces were expressionless masks, their eyes deep and pitiless. Something uneven crunched beneath my boots, and when I looked down, I discovered we walked a path made of crushed bones. I wondered if these were the victims of past years' sacrifices and if my bones would be joining these gory paving stones before the night was over.

But no. Best not to think of that. Best to look straight ahead and pretend they were only ordinary pebbles and stones I trod over.

A small hand shot out to touch my arm, startling me. The Skeltai child didn't grab me or try to slow my progress. She just stared up at me with large, serious eyes over shockingly hollow cheeks and trailed her fingers wonderingly down my skin—as pale as hers—as I passed by. Perhaps she was unaccustomed to seeing one who appeared to share her ancestry sacrificed.

I looked ahead and realized the way was edged on either side by outthrust hands reaching to touch us or bits of our clothing as we made our final walk. I guessed this was customary, but the touch of so many cold, unfamiliar hands was disturbing. When I whipped my head around again in search of the child's face, so disturbing in its emaciation it stirred even me to pity, it was gone, swallowed in a sea of more thin white faces.

These people were on hard times, I realized. So many looked half-starved. It was no wonder they believed they were out of favor and needed to appease their gods.

I looked past the wall of human bodies on either side of our ragged procession and ahead to what awaited us. A high platform of stone stood above the ground, taller than the heads of the onlookers and accessible by a wide set of steps leading to the top. The great platform was wide enough to accommodate dozens. A canopy of green leaves and willow fronds had been woven in a wood frame to shelter one area, and beneath this stood a solemn row of six men.

The shamans of the tribes. I somehow knew that without being told. Wearing feathered robes and hideously decorated headpieces of animal skulls, they were hardly recognizable as men and not beasts. They held scepters of wood and bone with the dried heads of small animals affixed to the tips, and their bodies were painted scarlet, not even a glimpse of pale skin visible beneath.

They made a ghastly sight lining the head of the steps, their nightmarish features lit intermittently orange and black by the flickering light of the bonfires. It wouldn't take much imagination to believe they weren't mere mortals but horrifying beings conjured from the depths of another world.

One of the shamans signaled our guards, and I found myself being cut free of the rope that bound me to the rest of the prisoners.

Was this it then? Was I to be the first to die? I squared my shoulders, but inside I was trembling as I was herded forward by a pair of Skeltai and pushed up the steps. I stumbled as I climbed up to the platform, and one of my guards caught me before I tumbled.

"Thank you," I said, struck by the incongruity of thanking one who was helping me to my death.

The savage inclined his head, and I wondered if I was imagining the flash of respect in his eyes. Surely so. How could he feel respect for someone he was about to slaughter like an animal? Yet now that I cast out my magic sense, I felt it in all of them, the surrounding spectators. It was there in their silence, their solemn gazes. It was the kind of reverence you sensed at the burial of a good man or the stillness of a sickroom where a friend lay dying. But I was no friend of these people. I was an enemy, a sacrifice for their bloodthirsty gods.

The bow, still slung over my shoulder though I had no arrows, burned warm on my back. It came to me then. The admiration these people felt wasn't for Ilan of Dimmingwood. It was for the bearer of the bow. The barra-banac.

I looked back at the upturned faces of the audience, wondering if I could use my newfound status to save myself. But my guards shoved me onward.

When I reached the top step, the shamans emerged from their willow-woven canopy and surrounded me. I looked into their nightmarish faces and tried to slow the pounding of my heart. They were men of flesh and blood, no matter how their paint and feathers suggested otherwise. I recognized the old shaman I had previously spoken with among them. It was he who placed himself directly before me.

"You come to offer us the barra-banac?" he asked.

I stared. Why had he pretended not to speak my tongue before? To throw me off balance?

Recovering from my surprise, I said, "You know I haven't come to deliver the bow. I told you before I've no intention of handing it over."

The old shaman's eyes revealed nothing, but I sensed my answer wasn't unexpected.

He was quick for an old man. In a flash, a narrow-bladed knife appeared in his hand and he pressed it against my throat. My guards grabbed me, their strong hands leaving me helpless to shrug an inch to either side, even had I been foolish enough to try it.

The shaman's voice was level, as if we had exchanged pleasantries as he said, "You think about it, kinswoman. Maybe change your mind?"

I resisted the urge to swallow, feeling the pressure of the sharp blade poised to slice into my skin. It was an effort to speak as if it wasn't there.

"My decision is made," I said. "You would use the bow to destroy the people of the provinces—*my* people. Death is preferable to placing so powerful a weapon into your hands."

I held my breath, feeling the pressure on the knife deepen. The shallowest of cuts opened on my skin, wetness trickling from the wound and down my collar. I kept my expression smooth and met the shaman's stare, eye to eye. Neither of us was going to give way.

Another shaman stepped up. He was a big fellow, a head taller than his companions and the only one of them who didn't look as if he had lived through a hundred hard winters. The level of cruelty I sensed in him made the hairs on my arms stand stiff.

Addressing the crowd, the big man raised his voice in the Skeltai tongue. The old shaman translated for my benefit.

"My people of the feather and the hoof, this traitor to her ancestors, this holder of the magic bow, shows contempt for our ways and our gods. Although we would treat her as a lost sister, she refuses to embrace our traditions and to return the bow to its rightful people. So I say, let her serve us in another way. Let us make a sacrifice tonight that will surely please the gods more than the blood of all these insignificant cattle."

The speaker's eyes raked disdainfully over the Fists and other prisoners gathered below the steps.

"Tonight we offer the blood of the bow's bearer, and through her the life force of the first barra-banac himself."

Whispers of unease rippled through the crowd, and the big shaman held up his hands for quiet.

But at that moment, another form of disruption stirred the audience. People parted or were shoved aside to make way for a handful of Skeltai warriors who approached the dais, dragging along a battered and disheveled-looking prisoner. Despite his injuries, the new prisoner somehow managed to walk with a straight back and his head held high.

My heart sank as I recognized the brave figure.

Chapter Eight

"Terrac…"

I was hardly aware of the dismayed murmur escaping my lips until I felt the older shaman's sharp eyes on me. I quickly smoothed my expression to one I hoped didn't betray too great an interest in the fate of the newcomer. I watched as he was drawn forward. Some guttural words were exchanged between his captors and the other Skeltai guards, and I saw they were about to add him to the line of Fists.

But the old shaman interrupted the proceedings, calling out an order. Nobody translated for me, but whatever he said gave pause to Terrac's captors. Instead of attaching Terrac to the line of Fists, they dragged him up the steps and onto the platform.

"Wait a minute. What's going on?" I demanded of the old one, forgetting for a moment the need to seem unconcerned. "I thought sacrificing me was going to be the high point of the ceremony. What are you doing with him?"

No one paid any attention to my questions. The shamans were conferring with one another. The old one seemed to be the leader of the lot, and it was he who did most of the talking now.

When Terrac reached the top of the steps, I managed to catch his gaze for an instant. He smiled weakly as he was hauled past me, but I could see by the paleness of his face and the way he sagged between his captors that he was in pain. He had the look of one fighting to remain on this side of consciousness as he was taken directly to the stone altar at the heart of the dais.

"What's going to happen to him?" I repeated, sweat breaking out on my upper lip. I would have grabbed the old shaman's arm and forced him to answer me if my arms hadn't been pinned firmly behind me.

When the old one turned to face me, I detected a gleam of triumph in his eyes.

He said, "Your friend attempted to escape, I am told, and was then doubly foolish in returning with the hope of freeing the rest of you. For that mistake he has earned the honor of beginning the blood rites."

My stomach lurched, but I summoned what defiance I could. "No. Let it be me," I said. "What is the need of killing any of these others? Surely the bearer of the bow is a great enough sacrifice?"

The shaman bared sharp, yellow teeth. "I think not. Maybe when you see your friends die you will have a change of heart concerning our offer."

I knew he was toying with me. He knew full well what it would do to me to watch this particular prisoner die. It was not by accident Terrac had been chosen to go first. I cursed whatever foul magic let the savage see into my heart and mind. But I held my tongue. If only I could buy a little time, just a few minutes to form a plan…

But that opportunity wasn't given to me. As I stood heartsick and frozen to the spot, Terrac was tied across the altar.

The old shaman said to me, "Do not stand back. I think you will wish to miss nothing of what is to come."

He motioned my guards, and I found myself dragged forward to stand directly before the altar. I looked down on Terrac lying bound and helpless across the stone already stained dark with the blood of a thousand past sacrifices. His face was taut with pain, but he betrayed none of the fear he must have felt. His captors had removed his armor, exposing a bright patch of red spreading across his shoulder and the tear of a jagged wound beneath his ripped shirt.

The shamans ringed the six-sided altar, and each produced a long, jagged dagger. The old one raised his hands to the night sky and shrilled a short speech I couldn't understand. The audience answered with enthusiasm, the noise of stamping feet and animallike screams erupting into the night and echoing around the clearing.

When the head shaman made a sharp cutting motion, the crowd instantly stilled. The old one threw back his head and began a bone-chilling chant, that same chant we had first heard back in the cages. When he paused, the younger shaman next to him took up the song and was followed by a third, until the singing passed around the entire circle. Then silence descended. I felt the audience holding their breaths and realized I was holding mine.

The head shaman towered over Terrac, but his attention was on me, a question in his eyes.

If I intended to stop this, it must be now. I opened my mouth to speak the words that would stay his hand, to give away the bow. But then my gaze found Terrac's, and he looked at me as if there was no audience around us and no knife hovering over him.

Don't give them what they want. Hold firm.

I could almost hear his voice in my head. He didn't want me to give our enemies the means to destroy the province, not even if I could save his life by doing it.

So I swallowed my protest and pressed my lips tight.

The shaman hesitated no longer. His knife flashed, severing fingers from his victim's hand. Terrac screamed in pain, and I squeezed my eyes closed.

I tried to shut out everything around me. Clenching my jaw, I saw Terrac and myself swimming together in Dancing Creek and climbing the rocks near Boulder's Cradle. Terrac sitting on the grass helping me learn to write my letters. Terrac hunting alongside me and Brig. I summoned my magic to blot out the pain and impending death, even as I drew to mind another ordinary scene—the old campsite at RedRock, where Terrac and I had spent so much of our youth. I was atop a rock over the cave, looking down. For an instant I saw the familiar green clearing and campfire. Then suddenly I was soaring impossibly high, and it was no longer Dimmingwood spread out far below but a dark forest of strange, towering trees. At the heart of that black forest, I saw a clearing where a scene from a nightmare unfolded before my eyes.

A great stone altar stood before a crowd of people so tiny they seemed like ants. I saw a suffering figure stretched across that altar and a handful of evil little men bent over him, tormenting him with small, shiny blades. Beyond them waited dozens of other frightened captives bound together and awaiting the moment when they too would be led up those stone steps and bound across the bloody rock.

And there at the center of it all stood one lone figure, straight-backed and hard-faced, with a bow slung across her back. Somehow I knew she had the power to stop them all with a single word. But her mouth was shut tight, and no plea or command escaped her lips. Within her she contained the strength to end this horror, but she was either too stupid or too uncaring to employ it, choosing instead to wait. To watch as they killed him and then another prisoner and another until finally it would be her own life taken.

Watching that stupid young woman, I was outraged at her refusal to act. Her stubbornness disgusted me. I wanted to sweep her up in my hand and crush her, to snatch her up from where she was and bring her here, where I could... I could...

I could snatch them all up.

The flash of clarity broke through my anger. I was experiencing one of those magical rifts Hadrian and I had talked about. Somehow I had created this rift, had willed my mind back to Dimmingwood. What if I could take myself there in body and the other prisoners with me? In theory it was possible, but I had never used my magic for anything so big before. Breathing deeply and refusing to think of the consequences of failure, I commanded my mind back into my body. I felt my awareness floating like a feather on the breeze, carried down, down...

The stone dais was beneath my feet again. The Skeltai guards still held me pinned in place. Terrac was before me, and below I sensed the watching eyes of the other frightened prisoners. Mentally I swept them all up in my arms. Terrac, myself, the Fists, and the stolen villagers—even the shaman bent over Terrac with a knife because I didn't know how to separate what stood so close. I drew us all away from the torch-lit clearing, away from the heart of the Black Forest, and into a world of blasting wind and deep shadows.

There was a rushing sense of speed as we traveled through utter darkness. I didn't try to understand where we were or how we passed through this space. If I relaxed my concentration even for a moment, relinquishing my hold on the others, I might never summon the strength to gather them again. There were so many of us. I felt the bounds of my magic shrinking around me and, panicking, I did what I'd never done before, strained my power to its limit. I drew on the well of magic until I thought it would go dry if it didn't burn me out first.

But somehow I didn't let go. I held on until I had that image of RedRock Cave in Dimming firmly fixed in my mind again. I saw the cave and the little clearing with the cold stream dashing past. I breathed deeply and found the scent of pine in the air.

The ground beneath my feet grew solid. Not the solid of the stone platform in that other place, but the comforting and familiar feel of damp earth covered in leaves and twigs. The feel of home.

Chapter Nine

I was drained, utterly spent, and it was all I could do to remain on my feet, swaying slightly. Dizziness and nausea swept over me, the effects of overusing my magic. Looking around, I found myself surrounded by strange men, women and children. The woods villagers huddled together in groups, looking dazed and fearful. It hadn't yet come home to them that they were safely returned to their world.

The Fists were here too. Disoriented, robbed of their weapons, and with their faces cut and bruised, they looked considerably less fierce than they used to. But they were quick to assess the change in their situation, and already some were untying one another.

I had done it. I had brought us home. Murmurs of triumph and approval stirred at the back of my consciousness, but I wasn't ready to listen to them just yet. I was too exhausted to be swept away in the flood of relief and elation I should feel. It was a powerful thing to be facing certain death one moment and in the next to be snatched away and returned to safety. The woodsfolk weren't the only ones uncertain how to react.

Above me the leafy rooftop of Dimming swayed in the breeze, and to the east the first orange and gold streaks of dawn were lighting up the sky. I looked at the encroaching forest and the shadow of RedRock Cave looming out of the emerging grayness and realized I ought to be making plans for moving this body of frightened people back to the shelter of their villages. They had a terrible experience behind them, and more hardship lay ahead. There were dead to be mourned and homes to be rebuilt. As for me, there was the Praetor to be informed of all that had happened. I had best get to work.

I would settle these folk here at RedRock to rest and recover from their ordeal, and then I would go on to Selbius. Just thinking of the journey ahead made me heavy with weariness, but I forced my chin up and straightened my shoulders for the task. I would pick out a Fist or two to accompany me and leave the rest in charge of the rescued captives.

It wasn't until then that I realized Terrac wasn't among the Fists or the villagers. My heart twisted in sudden panic even as I whipped around, scanning the clearing in the half light, praying to see his tall figure just beyond that group of villagers or standing there at the edge of the trees. But he wasn't here. He was nowhere.

Had I left him behind in the Black Forest? Had I lost my grip on him in that dark place between this world and that? Was he floating alone out there somewhere, lost in nothingness, doomed to be trapped forever in an unknown plain of existence?

And then I saw him. He stood with his back to me at the edge of the stream. It was a scene that stirred up memories. I recalled as if it were just minutes rather than years ago the time I built a lean-to just there and nursed a dying priest boy back to health. I'd thought him annoyingly sanctimonious then, but there was a stubbornness to him I had admired right away and a hidden core of strength below his surface. It had just taken me a long time to discover it.

It didn't realize my feet carried me toward him until he turned at the sound of gravel crunching beneath my boots. He held his injured hand against him, blood from his missing fingers leaking onto his torn shirt. His face was pale, and he swayed weakly. But he knew me. I could tell by the joy that leapt to his eyes as he forced a faint smile that seemed to say, *you did it, Ilan. I knew you could.*

In that instant, several things happened at once. Something moved at the corner of my vision, and I picked up an extra life sense. Inside my head, the bow shouted *danger*.

But I was too slow to move.

A Skeltai savage, the old shaman, was at the edge of the clearing. I remembered inadvertently transporting him here with us. A lethal weapon of magic hovered over his fingertips—a ball of heat and flame that would pierce flesh like a blade and burn through the vital organs with swift agony.

Terrac saw the same thing I did—the weapon aimed at me and me powerless to stop it. My magic was spent, and even my body betrayed me, refusing to attempt a physical dodge from the death about to be hurled at me.

Terrac leapt into action, throwing himself between me and the shaman.

Something came over me then. I saw the shaman's eye fall on Terrac, knew with certainty that in the next breath, the magic would be released that would drop my friend as surely as a bow shot. My world jerked to a halt, thought and reason abandoning me, as sheer instinct took over. I had always imagined that in such a defining moment, with everything on the line, some inner part of me would take over, that Ilan, the Hound, and all the other pieces that made up me would fall away, and I would simply do what I had been raised to do. Fight.

But instead panic took over. I lunged forward even as I opened my mouth to scream a hopeless warning. If the words came out, I never heard them. My heartbeat filled my ears, joined by the heavy thrum of powerful strains of magic being released to vibrate through the air. In my fear I released a magical weapon of my own, although I had no idea what or how. It was as if some other presence was responsible for the action and not me at all. No time to wonder. Fear filled me with one aim, to protect Terrac. There was no why or how, only this thing that must be done at any cost.

The few feet between us might as well have been a chasm. I knew even as I dived toward Terrac that I couldn't reach him in time. I saw him waver from an invisible blow just before I slammed into him, hurling us both to the ground. My immediate instinct was to shield my friend, and so I blanketed him with my body, part of me knowing already it was too late.

Terrac lay limp in my arms as I curled over him. I closed my eyes, rested my forehead against his chest, and waited, uncaring, for the next volley of enemy magic that would destroy us both.

Only it didn't come. I waited for death, but it was denied me. Terrac grew heavier in my arms. Every moment, I became more aware of how still he was, how lifeless and breathless. And still no merciful darkness came to banish my pain.

With trembling limbs, I shoved unsteadily to my feet, one thought pounding through my brain. For killing my Terrac, the shaman must die.

But when I looked for the magic wielder, I discovered I was to be denied my vengeance. He already sprawled upon the ground, victim to that mindless flash of raw magic I had instinctively hurled at him moments ago.

Eyes stinging, I swallowed the boulder that seemed to be jammed in my throat. I dropped to my knees and huddled beside my friend's motionless body, waves of grief pulling me under. I gave in to the aching loss, weeping loudly until my throat was raw and there were no more tears left.

When I could draw a steadying breath, I looked up with red eyes at the Fists and villagers crowded around.

The bow burned warm on my back, but I ignored its calling. Somehow I felt it was responsible for everything. It had changed me, had directed the course of my life, costing me the closest friend I'd ever had. No—he was more than a friend. I had loved him. My lips drew back in a bitter smile as I imagined what mockery he would have offered that little piece of information had he lived to hear it. Of course, without his death, it would never have been admitted…

"Erm, miss…?" one of the onlooking Fists ventured hesitantly. At any other time, I would have been amused to receive such a civil address from a Fist.

Realizing how demented I must look to him and the others—worse, how weak I surely appeared—I shoved my hair back from my face and scrubbed the tear streaks from my cheeks.

"Yes, what is it?" My voice, hoarse with emotion and rough from weeping, came out harsher than I intended. The Fist took a step back.

I remembered then that my actions today had surely identified me as a magicker. I could expect to be treated with fear from now on. At least until someone got around to killing or imprisoning me for possessing the forbidden talent.

"It's the under-lieutenant…" The Fist gestured uncertainly toward Terrac.

I looked where he indicated, and my heart stopped. Terrac's chest was rising and falling. I didn't know how, but it was. I put my ear to his chest and caught the faint thudding sound of a heartbeat beneath his ribs.

Suddenly there was hope in the world again. But I mustn't get too excited yet. He showed no signs of waking, and he might slip away at any moment. A memory flashed through my mind of a time I had delved into the consciousness of Garad, an injured outlaw, and had lent him some of my strength. I tried to remember how I had done it as I reached inward to gather my talent.

But I stopped short in surprise on finding none there. I had expended my last shreds of magical strength to destroy the shaman. Even my life sense was gone. I couldn't feel Terrac's presence near me or the warm glow that should have come from the dozens of strangers at my back.

It was no good trying to help him this way. I had no choice but to resort to healing in the only way I had ever had much success. I ripped up his shirt and swiftly used the strips to bind the bloody flesh of his hand. If I didn't put a stop to the flow of blood soon, it would kill him before the shaman's magic had the chance. I issued orders as my hands flew.

"You there," I snapped at the nearest Fist, "break up some pine boughs and get to work constructing a shelter beside the stream."

As he leapt to do my bidding, others gathered around to watch me work. I told a second man, "Go into that cave. You'll find it's been inhabited in the past. There should be all sorts of debris in there, and you can rummage around for some warm bedding and anything that might pass for healing supplies. We've got our work cut out for us keeping your lieutenant alive until we can get him to a qualified healer."

I couldn't see any sort of burn wound on Terrac from the shaman's magic, just the cuts and scrapes he had gained in Skeltai territory along with the missing fingers. One thing was sure, he would need more help than I could give him.

I said to the Fists, "Whichever of you is the fastest on foot and has the best head for direction needs to set out for Beaver Creek. If you don't find the Praetor and the other soldiers there, run all the way to Selbius if you have to. Don't waste any time or come back without the Praetor. And a healer."

I couldn't tell them why I was so desperate to have the Praetor here. I was hanging all my hopes on his magical powers of healing. But I wouldn't out him as a mage. Not yet. I was reserving that card for future use.

"Go on then, hurry!" I said.

They jumped into action and moved off in a huddle, bickering over who was to go for help and which of them would stay. Only one remained at my side.

"Help that other Fist get started on the shelter," I said.

He hesitated. "Wouldn't the under-lieutenant be more comfortable if we carried him into the cave?"

I contemplated Terrac's still form. "No, I don't think so," I said, remembering how Terrac had never liked the cave. "I have an idea if he's going to make it at all it'll be out here."

"If you say so."

The Fist disappeared, and for a while Terrac and I were left alone.

Chapter Ten

As the day played out, a strange calm descended on me. Almost as if I had seen and done all this before. I bathed Terrac's minor cuts and gashes, bandaging them as best I could. A handful of the woodsfolk women eventually worked up the nerve to approach with offers to help. I sent them out to gather healing herbs, not because I expected it to do any good, but to keep them out of the way. Terrac was fading fast, and I knew by nightfall his fate would be sealed one way or another.

I set more of the rescued prisoners to work cleaning out the cave in case we had to take shelter inside it that night. They labored with surprising energy, seemingly pleased to have familiar tasks to keep their hands busy. By midafternoon the women and children had a comfortable place to rest. A group of men went foraging for food in the woods, while others fished along the banks of the stream.

Like the rest of them, I sought to keep busy, to fill my mind with small things. Soon the Fist who I learned was called Burdel had raised a suitable shelter by the waterside.

He helped me move Terrac inside and onto a dry pallet that had been salvaged from the cave. There I sat watching my friend through the passing hours, waiting for him to miraculously open his eyes.

After a time I began talking to him, more to comfort myself than in the belief he could actually hear me, whispering all the soothing reassurances I could think of, hollow though they sounded. They were only stupid, useless words, the kind of nonsense you murmur to a child with a skinned knee. But I hoped if my voice reached wherever he wandered in the darkness, it would be something for him to take hold of and cling to until help arrived.

So I told him how afraid I was when I thought I had lost him so many times back in the Skeltai forest. I said how I admired his courage in coming back and attempting to rescue us, even though he had failed and even though, as I firmly told him, it had been a foolish thing to do. When I finished scolding him, I even told him the discovery I had made when I thought him dead—that I was in love with him. It was strangely easy to say that as he lay quietly sleeping, oblivious to my words.

The hours crawled by, and I was forced to conclude our messenger had gotten lost in the woods. Fists never could tell a sapling from an elder tree. I should have gone myself, but how could I leave Terrac alone?

I was waiting for my magic to return, testing it every hour to see if it was back. But I remained drained of the talent. Hadrian had once warned me it was possible to drain yourself so thoroughly the magic would take days to return, if recovery came at all. Was that what I had done then? Burnt the magic out of me forever? It seemed a betrayal to my mother's memory to say I didn't care if I had. Yet just now it was difficult to feel concern for anything but Terrac.

There was no physical injury from the shaman's magic. I had searched Terrac's body and found multiple bruises and minor injuries, but nothing that would account for his current state. I could only guess that my outflung magic during that awful moment had countered the shaman's spell. Rather than killing Terrac, the combined forces had sent his mind reeling out of his body. If the two couldn't be joined again soon, the body couldn't go on living much longer. Already it was failing, and without my magic, I was helpless to slow the downward spiral.

The day crept on until dusk darkened the sky. A chill crept into the air around us and I knew it was only going to grow colder as the night progressed. Sometime during the dark hours, Terrac was going to drift off into a deeper sleep from which he would never wake, and I was powerless to prevent it.

Drawing the heavy fur blanket up to his chin, I snuggled down on the earth beside him. I rested my hand on his chest so I could feel its rise and fall, offering myself both the comfort of knowing it continued for a little while yet and the anguish of feeling it grow shallower with each passing minute. We weren't far from the end now.

From outside came a distant commotion and the shuffle of approaching footsteps, but locked within a world of misery, I ignored them. Terrac's breathing stopped, and he fell perfectly still in my arms. Burying my face in the blanket, I finally let loose the tears I had been holding in.

There was a rustling sound as someone crawled into the shelter with us. I knew who it was without looking up.

"You're too late," I choked out. "He's already gone. Even you can't heal death."

Brow puckering, the Praetor pushed me aside and knelt to press black-gloved fingertips against the side of Terrac's neck. "What do you know of the powers at my disposal?" But it was an absent question. His focus was all on Terrac.

"You're wasting your time," I repeated bitterly. "I know a dead man when I see one."

"Maybe. But the condition you ignorant woods rabble call dead isn't always the real thing."

Before I could jerk away, he grabbed my hand and pressed it to the pulse point on Terrac's neck.

"Feel that?" he asked.

I felt it. The flutter was faint but definitely real.

"How can this be?" I gasped.

The Praetor ignored my question and spread his hands above Terrac's heart. His lips moved in a soft incantation I caught only snatches of. Whatever invisible magic he was using, it worked. Terrac sucked in a sudden gasp of air and heaved it out again. I leaned my face closer to his, ignoring the Praetor's instructions to keep out of the way.

"Terrac, can you hear me?" I whispered.

The only response was a flicker of his eyelids. But at least he was breathing again, the strong, steady breath of one who sleeps a healthy sleep.

"Get back, foolish girl. Give him some air," the Praetor commanded, and I obeyed this time.

"He was dead," I said disbelievingly. "I don't understand what happened."

"Of course you don't. Brilliant men with twice your years and intellect wouldn't comprehend it."

Too dazed to take offense, I said, "But he wasn't breathing. His heart had stopped. How did you bring him back?"

Was it my imagination or did the Praetor hesitate before letting out an exaggerated sigh?

"Very well," he said. "I suppose a young woman of your background knows how to keep a secret. If you don't, just remember all I hold over you, and perhaps that will keep you discreet."

"I'm as silent as the grave," I said quickly, thinking of Fleet in his prison cell and Terrac now fully at the mercy of this man.

"Then suffice to say both the damage to Terrac and the healing of him were a matter of magic. A powerful spell was slowly drawing the life from him. Soon his carcass would have been an empty shell. As a mage, I was able to find Terrac's still-lingering essence and tug it back into his body. If he had been dead longer than a moment, it would have been impossible, as his life force would have moved on to some other place."

"I see," I said.

"I doubt it. What would a forest mongrel like you know of such things?"

He briskly examined the bandages I had placed over Terrac's shallower wounds, saying, "All he needs is rest and plenty of fluids when he wakes. You shouldn't get much food into him for the next day or two, but when his appetite does return, it'll be doubled. After that, he'll be back on his feet again."

He checked another bandage. "You did all right with these, I suppose."

I knew by the way he said it he had expected to find otherwise.

I ignored the dubious praise and said, "Won't you do something about his fingers? Can't those be magically healed too?"

He unbound Terrac's injured hand and looked for the first time on the wound.

"No, I can do nothing for these," he said, neither his expression nor his tone betraying any emotion. "Take care of them as best you can. Keep the cut clean and packed with earthleaf to protect it from infection. That should be simple enough, even for you."

He deftly rebound Terrac's injured hand as skillfully if it were a task he had accomplished a hundred times before.

He continued flatly. "The boy was lucky. His sword hand is undamaged, so he can still be of use to me. And the thumb of the bad hand is preserved, so he'll soon adjust to the missing digits."

"You really don't care about him, do you?" I realized. "For all you believe Terrac is your own flesh and blood, the offspring of your brother, he's nothing more to you than a useful tool, a soulless piece in your greater game. His suffering doesn't matter, only his fitness to serve you."

I was angry enough not to care if I tread on dangerous ground. "If he had died here tonight, you wouldn't have mourned his death, only the inconvenience that brought you all this way for nothing."

The Praetor grimaced at the blood smeared on his gloves. "What do you know about my brother, Habon?" he asked quietly.

I should be afraid when his voice had that edge to it. I knew that. But I couldn't seem to care about the consequences of my outburst.

"Do you take me for a fool?" I asked. "Do you think I don't know the significance of the brooch he wears, bearing the Fidelity and Service motto of the house of Tarius? I did a little research on you during my time in Selbius. No one but one of your blood would have access to that brooch. And no one in your house is unaccounted for but your long-lost brother."

"Habon was not lost. He was disgraced," the Praetor cut me off. "My brother made an… unwise decision, for which I had no choice but to disinherit him."

"Because he pursued a woman of humble origins and poor ancestry," I said.

"Because he loved a witch descended from the very pale savages who torment the province now," he countered. "When he chose her over his duty, he became an enemy of the province."

"And brought your wrath down on all magickers," I said. "But then Terrac showed up a dozen years later with the brooch. I suppose your wrath had cooled by then."

"Justice had been satisfied by the death of his parents and the destruction of every magicker I could get my hands on," the Praetor corrected. "Guessing the boy's parentage, I saw fit to show him mercy."

It was on the tip of my tongue to tell him I and not Terrac was the offspring of his brother and the "witch." But then I looked down on Terrac's sleeping face. He looked peaceful now and much younger, like the boy I remembered. Maybe by keeping silent on this matter, I could keep him safe.

"You brought him up at the keep under your protection," I mused. "That's why he was trained with the Fists and promoted at so young an age to under-lieutenant, third down from the top of command. You had plans for him."

"I foresaw he might have his uses one day. Much like you."

I clenched my teeth. It was bad enough to hear him speak so of Terrac, but I was unaccustomed to being treated as if I had no thoughts or feelings of account.

"I hope you got all you needed from me," I said. "Because I'm no longer yours to command. Find yourself a new instrument."

He feigned surprise, saying, "I am disappointed. Are you forgetting your vows of service so quickly?"

"I have forgotten nothing. Those cursed vows have never been far from my mind since the moment I took them. I'm not one to break my word. Which is why you are going to break it for me. You're going to release me from my oath."

"Am I?" he sounded amused. "And after I went to such trouble to procure it. Tell me, my ignorant forest friend, why should I do such a thing? Your services have proven invaluable already. I'd be a fool to cast them aside."

"You'd be a greater fool to hold close to you an enemy who knows the secret that could lead to your downfall, the secret you will do anything to keep from seeing the light of day."

"Truly? That sounds intriguing. What is this dangerous mystery I'm so desperate to conceal? I know you do not speak of my exploration of the art of magic. Because that's not the sort of accusation I'm likely to admit before witnesses."

"I don't need you to," I pointed out. "The merest breath of rumor will be enough to cause your downfall. And the beauty of it is it will have been brought about entirely by your own law. It was you who declared the practice of such magic punishable by death."

"Yes. That was before I realized the talent could be learned, not merely inherited. It was then I recognized its fascinating potential in the right hands."

"Meaning yours alone."

He shrugged. "It would be unwise to allow such a weapon to be wielded randomly."

A muscle in my cheek twitched. "So you wanted to eliminate competition?" I asked, my voice coming out so cold I hardly recognized it. "My family died so you could be the only one to possess the shiny new talent you'd discovered?"

I didn't give him a chance to respond as I rushed on. "My mother and father were magickers. They were killed, murdered before my eyes, during the cleansing you ordered all those years ago."

"Heartbreaking," he said dryly. "Unfortunately this means you also carry the strain of magic—not something I would admit to openly, were I you."

"I'm not finished yet." At this point, I was beyond feeling fear. Speaking of my parents had brought up old memories and the anguish I had only imagined healed. The pain had been put away and forgotten for a long time but never dealt with.

I said, "A single whisper to the wrong person, a moment's gossip with some fishwife along the docks. That's all it would take for word of your magery to get out. I have no fear for my hide. I've worn it long enough already. But you value your life and your power. I don't think you'd enjoy giving up either."

"Enough." The Praetor looked at me distastefully. "Clearly you're quite mad." He titled his head to one side. "I could have you silenced and all your vermin friends with you. I think I would enjoy that."

Under his gaze I felt a stir of unease and wondered if I had miscalculated my position.

"It would be so easy," he continued. "I would not even have to employ an executioner. With my magic, I could just reach right here into your chest."

His fingers hovered over my heart. "I could close an invisible fist, and with one tight squeeze you would never trouble me again."

My heart beat faster, as if already feeling the pressure of an unseen hand. I struggled to keep fear from my face.

"But you won't do it," I said with more confidence than I felt. "If you wanted me dead, I'd be a corpse already."

He dropped his hand away, and I breathed a sigh of relief as he admitted, "Alas, you are right. I haven't any intention of disposing of you right now. Something holds me back. I have the strangest feeling there is unfinished business between you and me—and him."

He looked past me to Terrac's sleeping form. "There is a future yet undecided."

I narrowed my eyes. I wanted nothing to do with this man who was my uncle or any future plans he might lay.

But aloud I only said, "You were about to release me from my oath."

The hint of a smile tugged at his lips. "You're a single-minded young woman, aren't you? Courageous, I am told, and a force to be reckoned with. You've even impressed my men. And now here you stand… defying me. Perhaps you should have been of my blood and not the disappointing young under-lieutenant here."

I held my peace. No need for him to know how dry the back of my mouth was or how shaky my insides.

"Very well," he said. "It pleases me to grant your request. But be warned. This battle is far from over."

I didn't like the sound of that.

When he placed his palm on my forehead, his skin was cold to the touch, and I felt the bite of the ring of his ancestors pressing against my brow.

He said, "I hereby release you from my service. You may go your own way, severed from all vows or obligations, for the space of a year and a day."

I rocked backward. "What is this about a year and a day? What sort of release is that?"

"It is the best bargain you are going to get," he said. "I advise you to accept it. I expect we can do without you until next winter. The Skeltai savages will settle down now that their pagan holiday is past for another year. We've unsettled them, striking back as we did, and now that they know we're not easy prey, they may let us be altogether."

I frowned. "I don't see how you can be so certain of that."

"Let us just say I have learned the skill of foresight. Enough so to see I shall have no immediate need for you here."

I felt a little queasy, wondering what else he had seen in the future.

He gave me no opportunity for questions. "But on the day after this, one year hence, I expect you to return to my service and take up whatever duties I see fit to set before you."

My jaw tightened. "That's not the freedom I demanded."

He smiled thinly, an expression that held no warmth. "There are other small favors I'm prepared to offer. Such as a pardon for your crimes and those of your circle of thieves. Each of you may walk among ordinary folk, may leave this shaded wood without fear of capture or punishment."

I choked on my rage, and not all of my anger was directed at my enemy. I had thought myself so clever. I had imagined my plans well laid. And yet he had caught me up in them with as little effort as a spider capturing an unwary insect. He watched me now, waiting for my answer.

"Do we have a bargain, thief?" he asked.

"Do I have a choice?"

"Not really."

"And what of him?" I nodded toward Terrac.

The Praetor shrugged. "What of him? He will travel back to Selbius with us in the morning. He'll sleep like a babe, most likely, even on horseback. The kind of healing I employed is strength-sapping, for sufferer and healer alike. Once he's home again, he'll be back on his feet and returned to his old duties within the week. Perhaps some new ones as well. His superior, my lieutenant of Iron Fists, was killed in the fighting at Beaver Creek. My captain believes this boy is level-headed and resourceful enough to take his place, and I'm inclined to agree with him."

He looked at me as if he knew something of what was on my mind. "It is what the boy wants. Believe me, not for anything would he give up the opportunity to be the captain's second."

"I suppose not," I said aloud. Were my feelings really so transparent? But at least Terrac would live, I thought, watching his chest rise and fall. Whatever became of me and whatever future or freedom I was forced to give up, at least one of us had come through right in the end. Who'd have thought it would be Terrac rather than me? And who'd have thought I wouldn't want it any other way?

I turned to inform the Praetor I agreed to his terms but he had already gone, slipping quietly into the dark night. No need to tell him what he already knew.

I knelt and resettled Terrac's blankets. For a moment the urge had been so strong. Frighteningly strong. I could have opened my mouth and spilled out another truth to the Praetor, one he hadn't heard before. That Terrac was not his nephew. Perhaps it would have shaken him, discovering he didn't after all grasp the situation he imagined himself in such firm control of. But to do that would have been to deny Terrac his opportunities. The Praetor would withdraw his support, maybe casting Terrac out of his place among the Fists, and then my friend would return to the futureless, impoverished state he had sprung from. Only this time I couldn't imagine he would have enough hope for the future to sustain him.

Terrac stirred in his sleep, and I realized he was waking. I repositioned myself so my face would be the first thing he saw when he opened his eyes.

"Ilan… is it you?" He blinked and rubbed his good hand shakily across his face as if just waking from a deep night's slumber. But I could tell by the weakness in his voice and the carefulness of his movements that the healing had left him far more drained than any ordinary sleep. His words confirmed it.

"Are we safe?" he asked. "Because I don't think I could summon the strength to crawl away even if another savage was coming straight at me."

I smiled, trying to seem ordinary, although I felt a strange tight sensation at the back of my throat at hearing his voice when I had thought never to hear him speak again. "Yes, we're safe now. The Skeltai shaman who injured you is dead. For a time we feared for your life, but the Praetor came and looked after you, and now you're past all danger."

"The Praetor?" He gasped. "He's here?"

He made a feeble move as if to sit up, and I pushed him down again, easy to do since he hadn't the strength to lift himself more than inches from the ground.

"He's outside somewhere. Forget about him. He's seen you, pronounced you whole enough to remain of use, and said you would be fit to travel in the morning."

"Whole enough?" He looked down at his bandaged hand. "Oh yes. I'd almost convinced myself it was only a dream."

I tried to sound comforting but not *too* comforting because I knew pity would not be welcome. "It's not so bad," I said. "As the Praetor pointed out, it isn't your sword hand. You should still get by well enough without it. You'll just need some time to adjust to the change."

I forced a smile, knowing matters were not as simple as I made them sound. I could only imagine how he felt knowing he would spend the rest of his life less than whole.

"Not so bad…," he repeated quietly, his eyelids half-closing. I could see he wanted to rest again, but I made him drink a little water before I left him.

Then I crawled out of the shelter and into the cold night. The stream babbled nearby, and overhead the treetops stirred in the wind. It was good to be home again. Almost good enough to drive away all my worries. But not quite.

A blazing campfire had been lit nearby, and the lost villagers gathered around it, talking softly over the meager meal they had managed to scrounge up. Mothers rocked small children in their arms, and many folk sprawled out in the shadows beneath the trees at the clearing's edge because the cave wasn't large enough to hold them all.

The Praetor had brought a large contingent of fighting men with him. I judged them to be the same soldiers we had left near Beaver Creek when we stepped into the portal and the horrors that awaited us on the other side. I never thought the sight of a Fist would bring me any feeling of security, but it did now. The Fists who had come through our shared ordeal mingled with their fellows, but they were quiet, as if they couldn't yet believe they were safe and had lived to tell of their adventure.

The thought of joining either villagers or Fists didn't tempt me. I was in the heart of the woods, and solitude beckoned. So I slipped off on my own—but not too far, lest Terrac have need of me.

I climbed to the top of RedRock and sat on a ledge jutting out over the falls. The water gushed past with a roar that blotted out the more distant noise of the folk below. A fine veil of mist sleeked my skin, but I didn't move back. Perhaps a little cold would help shock me back to my senses. They were certainly in sore need of wakening at this point.

What was I going to do about Terrac? In a perfect world, once he recovered, all our troubles would be over. He would abandon his new life, voluntarily leaving the Praetor's service, and the two of us could go away someplace where our enemies would never find us. Someplace where we didn't have to worry about recurring Skeltai raids or the Praetor's personal battles or secrets of the past coming back to haunt us. Was there such a place for a one-time outlaw and a would-be priest boy?

I snorted. It was all foolishness. A ridiculous dream, no less, and one I would have to get over. Sometimes dreams had to take second place in the face of cold reality. Terrac would go on being what he was and I… What would become of me? After a year and a day I would be honor bound by my word to return to a lifetime of following the Praetor's bidding.

There was a scraping sound on the rocks nearby.

"Hope this ledge doesn't give way." Dradac had to raise his voice to be heard over the rush of the waters as he settled on the rock beside me.

"It will with a giant like you plunking his weight down on it," I said. I scooped up a handful of loose pebbles and tossed them over the edge into the rushing falls. We shared a companionable silence for a while.

"How'd you get here?" I asked at last.

"Same way you did. I climbed."

I smiled slightly. "You know what I mean."

He said, "A better question might be how did the Praetor and his fancy soldiers get here?"

"So it was you who led them to us," I realized. "I wondered whatever became of that messenger I sent."

"Nothing good if we hadn't found him. We discovered the fellow wandering like a lost lamb in the heart of the wood. Just going in circles, he was. It was pitiful to see. Considering how he was one of the Fists we knew had been with you, we figured whatever he was about might be important enough for us to step in and give a hand. He was that grateful when we led him to the camp the Praetor set up along Beaver Creek. And of course when the fellow described where he'd come from and how swift help was needed, we led them all back over our old grounds."

I nodded. "Feels strange to be back here, doesn't it? Almost like we never left. All we need is Rideon and the rest of the band, and it'd be just like the old days. Except for the extra company."

"And unlikely company the Praetor and a contingent of Fists would be if the Hand were around," he said.

"What do you hear of him these days?"

"I still have friends among the band. I think they get on all right." He studied the palms of his hands. "But you didn't really come up here to think over old times, did you?"

When I kept silent, he asked, "You need to be alone now?"

"Yeah," I admitted. "I think I do."

When he was gone, I slipped the bow from my back. As if sensing some hint of my intentions, it warmed, humming to life in my hands. And there it was again, that sibilant whisper tickling at the back of my consciousness.

You cannot rid yourself of me. All we have gained was accomplished together. You are nothing without me. Nothing.

With an effort, I unclenched my jaw enough to say, "Maybe nothing is what I prefer to be. When I was nothing, I was free and my will was my own. The decisions I made might be right or wrong but at least they were mine."

The bow fell silent, but it glowed still hotter in my hands, becoming uncomfortable to hold onto. That was all right. It only made what I had in mind that much easier.

Closing my eyes, I cast the bow out from me, flinging it as far over the stone's edge as it could fly. I had no idea which direction it went, nor did I want to know. There was a tingling sensation in the back of my mind as the weapon slipped away.

And then it was gone.

Suddenly I was alone inside my head, the isolation sharply unfamiliar. I realized then how completely under the power of the bow I had been. I hadn't known the extent of its intrusion until it was absent.

I collapsed to my knees and drew a quivering breath. Relief washed over me, but there were other emotions mixed in as well. Hope and doubt warred with one another. Had I done the right thing? And if so, why did I feel empty? Why did this newfound sense of freedom come with an echo of regret?

I bit my lip.

It will pass. I will forget you, bow. In time.

I opened my eyes and looked out into the night. Faint streaks of gray were beginning to lighten the sky. Below me the shadowed forms of the forest trees swayed gently in the wind, and Dimmingwood stretched its green mantle as far as the eye could see.

Chapter Eleven

There was just one other thing I had to do before departing with Hadrian for the mystical hills of Camdon.

The sky was streaked with the semilight of early dawn, the air crisp with the kind of chill that leaves a tingle in the lungs. A stiff winter wind cut through the market square, and I lifted my hood as I entered the gathered throng around the east end, less as a shield against the wind than for the purpose of hiding myself from curious eyes.

I could scarcely walk anywhere in the city since the day of the Praetor's pardon without being recognized and hailed by the citizens. Their gratitude seemed genuine, but I was uncomfortable under the attention of so many. Their praise made me ill at ease because I wondered how many of them would willingly have cheered at my hanging only a few days ago when I was still an acknowledged outlaw. Besides, today wasn't a day for congratulations.

I turned a shoulder and slid through the crowd as silently as a fish slipping through dark waters. There was a strange restlessness about the audience, but no one pushed or shoved, and every voice was hushed. I felt a ripple move through the gathering as I made my way forward. Beyond the crowd I glimpsed snatches of color, the crimson and midnight of the Fists' uniforms as they passed by. The chink of metal armor and the ring of heavy boots echoed across the cobblestone pavement. As one, the crowd strained forward, craning their necks for a view of the escort and their prisoner.

I hung back, clinging to the shadows along the edge of a market stall, inwardly continuing the battle I had thought already decided when I first donned my cloak and slipped outdoors before dawn. How long had I paced the confines of Hadrian and Seephinia's tiny hut on the river barge, railing at the fate that had brought this story to such an inevitable end? How long had I questioned my intentions in coming here? Was it satisfaction at my victory, a desire to look into his eyes and let him see that just once it was I who would walk away in triumph? Did a cold part of me want to gloat at such a moment?

I hated to think anything that low could drive me, but my feelings were a confused mass even I couldn't untangle. All I could be certain of was that whatever initially carried me forward, I took no pleasure now in putting one foot in front of the other, moving deeper into the throng. Roughly, I forced my way through the tightly packed spectators, causing a few exclamations and muttered oaths until the offended parties caught a glimpse of my face. Then they fell utterly silent and stood aside. I saw one person turn to another, and like wild flames, a whisper spread through the crowd.

It's her! She is here! Of course she would be...

I closed my ears to the murmurs and tried not to feel their stares settle over me. Toward the forefront of the crowd I caught sight of my object.

He was being led up a set of long wooden stairs onto a high platform just above the heads of the crowd. A brawny Fist flanked him on either side with iron-gauntleted fists clamped firmly on both his arms. Their presence was unnecessary. He neither struggled nor sagged in defeat between his escorts, but carried himself easily, defiance gleaming from jewel-green eyes shot with glints of fire. For a lifetime those eyes had hypnotized everyone who looked into them, compelling a loyalty kings might have envied. They'd drawn me to the very brink of destruction more than once in my overwhelming eagerness to win one look of approval.

And I never had.

It was with a sinking stomach that I watched him ascend the steps to the scaffold. A man in long robes opened a thick scroll to read the listed crimes of the condemned man to the crowd. As if there were any need to do that. As if there was so much as a child in our midst who had not heard of Rideon the Red Hand and couldn't recite his misdeeds from memory.

I ignored the words of the official and focused my attention on the prisoner. He showed no hint of fear as a loop of rope was placed around his neck and the rough braid tightened around his throat. His eyes roved over the crowd with a chilling confidence as if it was he who waited to witness our execution instead of the reverse. The hint of a smile hovered around his lips as if he laughed at some private joke. As if he and only he were aware this entire plot was unfolding exactly as he had written it and we were the real dupes of the scene. I felt the crowd's unconscious response of mingled surprise and anger.

We waited in utter silence as the robed official fell silent, his last words ringing out over the stillness.

"...sentenced by the greatly merciful but ever-just Praetor Tarius to immediate death by hanging. Let no man pity the scoundrel or recount his past misdeeds. From this day forward, by the decree of the Praetor, to mention the very name of Rideon the Red Hand shall constitute an act of treason against the province and be punished as such."

Even the crowd seemed to think this a bit much. A few startled gasps erupted as, for a moment, their indignation turned from the convicted man to his oppressor. I wondered if they were remembering an earlier time when some had thought the Red Hand a hero of the common folk for daring to challenge their heavy-fisted ruler.

The executioners hurried with their task as if they could sense the opinion of the people swinging against them. The robed official, looking out at the stony faces turned upward, paled and proclaimed hastily, "If the condemned has any final words, the gracious Praetor will allow him to speak them."

The Praetor wasn't even present, but perhaps the nervous official hoped the prisoner would say something to persuade the crowd to accept his fate without a riot. He might better have feared a rousing speech calculated to incite violence. But neither came. Rideon the Red Hand was too good a player to an audience to ruin a tragic moment or a somber mood with mere words.

I felt sympathies rise higher in the face of his proud silence and arrogant gaze. Even in death it seemed the outlaw mocked his old enemy. He would be a martyr to these people, I realized suddenly, his death a rallying point for future revolt. And that was doubtless exactly how he had planned it.

After a prolonged hush, his executioners evidently decided they had been more than generous. Now they acted with rude haste to secure the prisoner's hands tightly behind his back before removing their own feet from the vicinity of the trapdoor. A uniformed Fist moved to the lever that would drop the floor. I sensed his eagerness at the task and knew with a flash of insight the Fists had fought over which of them would receive the coveted pleasure of drawing the lever that would plunge the outlaw to his death. Had Terrac been among them? Surely not. I didn't see him here today.

The question was blasted from my mind by a sudden bolt of emotion shooting through me like a hot arrow. Pride. Fear. Fury. Regret.

They weren't my emotions—they came from the man at the end of the rope. But for a moment they had been made mine. I hadn't sought Rideon out this final time, but somehow his life essence had touched mine, and despite the unpleasantness of the contact, I couldn't find it in me to shake it loose. On the surface Rideon remained aloof, head held high, feet planted wide, as if they stood confidently on firm forest ground, rather than hovering over a chasm of death.

But for a brief instant, my magic was stronger than it had ever been. I was one with him. Somehow, miraculously, his eyes dropped to find me unerringly in the crowd. Our gazes met and held. I discovered then what I had come for. I felt his flicker of surprise as he realized I was the last one standing after all the others had fallen, felt a grudging respect from him that warmed me at my very core. I was again the hungry hound who had waited so long to win my captain's recognition.

I sensed rather than saw the Fist's hand hovering over the lever.

Rideon's eyes left mine, lifting to gaze above the heads of the crowd and into the distance. Toward Dimmingwood. I watched his face take on a faraway look, saw his chest rise in a final intake of breath. And then, suddenly, he was gone. The platform dropped from beneath him with a sharp cracking noise. The rope went taut, the crowd held their breaths. And then it was all over.

I didn't linger after but turned abruptly and shoved my way through the crowd to exit the market square. I needed to get into the open air, needed to find some place where I could breathe again. I felt the rolling waves of the crowd's resentment breaking, heard the confused cries and threats from the Fists as the newly angry mob closed in. Too late the people realized their enemy had also been their champion. I didn't pause to look back as the fighting erupted. Violence hovered in the air of this city, and perhaps it would for a long time. But I wouldn't be a part of it today.

Today my captain was dead.

* * *

The following morning I left Selbius and all its bitter memories behind me. Hadrian, always the wanderer, had decided it was time to return to his travels. When invited, I leapt at my first opportunity to see something of the world beyond the province. So Hadrian and I said our farewells to the river folk—Seephinia took Hadrian's departure with the stoicism typical of her people, although I fancied her eyes were unusually bright. Perhaps I imagined it, but I thought she even seemed a little sorry to see the last of me. Strangely, I found that I returned the sentiment.

I felt a very real regret upon saying good-bye to Fleet, who was also present as we left the river barges. The fact that he had braved his sickness on the waters long enough to cross over and help us move our things off the river barge said much of how close our friendship had grown over our adventures together. We didn't speak of seeing one another again, but I thought as he gripped my shoulders in a friendly embrace and looked knowingly into my eyes that no words needed to be said. We would meet again. I was as certain of that as I could be of anything in this world.

Fleet had procured by some mysterious means an elderly and emaciated donkey to aid us on our trip by carrying the bulk of our traveling gear. And so we set out northward along the Selbius Road, embarking on the many weeks' journey that would eventually lead us to the province of Camdon.

I didn't feel any sense of loss at putting the Praetor or his city at my back. If only it were so easy to banish the memories of someone else I was leaving behind…

* * *

"What is it? Trouble?" Hadrian asked as I stiffened at his side and slowed my steps.

"No. It's nothing."

But my hands crept of their own accord toward the knives tucked up my sleeves.

"Is this 'nothing' anything to do with the dark stranger up ahead?"

Hadrian nodded toward a tall figure loitering beneath the signpost that marked the first branch in the Selbius Road. The stranger's hood was pulled up against the wind, the hem of his black cloak swirling around his boots. There was something secretive about him. He appeared to be waiting for something or someone.

"He's just another traveler," I said to reassure myself as much as Hadrian. "He's nothing to do with us."

I'd spent too much time running and fighting for my life lately. That was all. Paranoia made me jump at shadows, made me fearful of plots and betrayal at every innocent encounter. Even now, as I looked at this hooded stranger, I remembered the Praetor had executed innocent people in the past, people who were on his side. Who was to say he couldn't do it again?

As we drew nearer the fork in the road, the stranger turned his head away, concealing his features. The casual gesture made me think of a Praetor's spy. Or an assassin sent to ensure I didn't live long enough to enjoy the year of freedom the Praetor had promised. Had he had second thoughts about our deal? Decided he had no use for me after all? No one knew better than I that the man who was both my enemy and my uncle was capable of anything.

My mouth went dry. Without the bow, I felt suddenly helpless. With my weak knives alone, was I capable of protecting myself and Hadrian? With sweaty palms, I gripped the handles of my knives.

Hadrian must have sensed my jumbled emotions because he cleared his throat.

"In the interests of saving this poor fellow's life, I should probably mention he's no footpad, but an acquaintance of mine."

Relief washed over me. "You could have said as much."

"A thousand apologies. I met the fellow yesterday, and upon learning he intended to travel our way, I invited him to meet us outside the city and join our party."

I snorted. "Just what we need. I suppose your new friend is too frightened to travel alone? Concerned about thieves, is he?"

"Something like that." Hadrian's lips twitched. "Perhaps we should hasten to assure him he'll encounter no such scum while in our company."

I didn't respond to his banter. We were closer to the stranger now, and it struck me forcefully that there was something familiar in his height and bearing, in the shape of his shoulders and the glint of a sword revealed each time the wind tugged open his cloak. If his hood fell down, I wondered, would I recognize the familiar, stubborn set of his chin too?

No. It couldn't be.

Nevertheless, I felt myself moving forward and realized with the sound of my pounding feet that I was running.

"Terrac," I cried seconds before throwing myself into his arms with a force he could hardly have expected. He reeled back a few steps, and together we crashed into the signpost.

Laughing breathlessly, I clung to him.

"Whoa, there. Go easy on an injured soldier," he laughed, steadying himself as his hood fell back to reveal the teasing violet eyes I had come to love. "You know it was only days ago I was flat on my back, recovering from the Praetor's healing."

"So what are you doing here now? How did you get away? Are you sure you're recovered?"

He winced under the flow of words, but I didn't care as I grabbed his injured hand and examined the bandage critically.

"This is sloppy work," I said. "Our old healer Javen could have done better. But never mind. I'll soon fix it."

"I've no doubt you will," he said with a hint of amusement. "But the fingers are gone. Even you can't heal that. Not to worry though; the rest of me is good as new. At least it is now that I see you."

He cupped my chin affectionately in his good hand, but I wasn't ready to be distracted. Not yet.

"You haven't answered my questions. How did you get away from the Praetor? Don't tell me he released you willingly from his service?"

He tilted his head to one side. "There was no need for that. I simply reminded him what a valuable asset you'll be to the province in the event of any more trouble from the Skeltai and pointed out it would be a great loss to him if any harm befell you on your travels."

"A loss *to him*?" My breath caught. "You aren't saying you told him about…?"

"Of course not," he reassured me quickly. "The true relationship between you is for you to share if you ever decide to. Or for him to figure out for himself. It's not my secret to give away. Speaking of which…" He removed something shiny pinned to his collar. "This is not mine to hold on to either."

"My old brooch." A wealth of emotions flooded through me as he dropped it into my palm. I turned the brooch over, reading the inscription on the back. *Fidelity and Service.* The motto of the Praetor's family. Of *my* family.

For an instant, a memory came rushing back: my mama pressing the thing into my hand and telling me it would protect me. Maybe in a way it really had? At least it had protected the man I loved.

Terrac fastened the pin to my collar, and I realized he was still talking. "I suggested to the Praetor that it would be a shame if we were to lose you and your many skills to an attack of roadside brigands. Especially when such an inconvenience could be so easily prevented by sending one of his most trusted men to accompany you as a bodyguard."

"And he believed that? That I, of all people, need protection from brigands?" I tried to exchange a look of disbelief with Hadrian but my priest friend had hung back to grant us privacy.

Terrac said, "To tell the truth, I think he was more concerned you wouldn't honor your word to return at the allotted time. I have instructions to see that you do."

I narrowed my eyes, the old combative spirit stirring within me. "Will you now? I'd like to see you take me anyplace I didn't want to go."

"Then you're going to be disappointed because it's actually you who'll be taking me places. I met Hadrian yesterday and settled everything. I'm just an extra member of your party under orders to follow you to the ends of the earth, should you choose to visit them." He smiled. "Somehow I don't think I'll mind that."

And looking at him, I knew I wouldn't mind it either.

NOT AN ENDING, BUT A RESTING PLACE

I roll over, trying to find a position on the hard-packed earth where rocks and sticks won't dig into my flesh. Terrac sleeps, peaceful and oblivious at my back, emanating a warmth and sense of safety I don't think I'll ever grow fully used to. I smile, thinking how much I love him and wondering what the future holds for the two of us. It's still too dark in these early morning hours to see, but I hear Hadrian snoring heavily somewhere nearby. Another source of reassurance it may take me a while to grow accustomed to—that of a loyal friend.

It was all very hard at first. I worried about my magic and whether it would ever come back or if I had burned myself out forever in my battle with the Skeltai shaman. I wondered if I had done right in not telling the Praetor I was his blood kin. What if he ever found out the truth?

Most of all, every night like this spent camped alongside the road, I was tormented by dreams of Brig, Rideon, the Praetor... Often I would wake with a start and reach for my bow, always so close to my side. Only it wasn't there. Not anymore.

But by day the weight on my heart gradually grew lighter with each passing mile of our journey. I learned to be at peace with my questions, content to discover the answers if and when life led me to them. And then this morning came. I lie here waiting for dawn's first light to creep into the sky and I realize the old seductive whisper in my head, the voice of the bow, has faded to nothingness. At last all is still.

Continue Ilan's journey in Book V, Journey of Thieves.

ABOUT THE AUTHOR

C. Greenwood started writing stories shortly after learning her ABCs and hasn't put down her pen since. After falling in love with the fantasy genre more than a decade ago, she began writing sword and sorcery novels. The result was the birth of her best known works, the Legends of Dimmingwood series. In addition to her writing, Ms. Greenwood is a wife, mom and graphic designer.

Want to learn more about C. Greenwood or her books? Check out her website or "like" her on Facebook.

Legends of Dimmingwood Series

Magic of Thieves ~ Book I
Betrayal of Thieves ~ Book II
Circle of Thieves ~ Book III
Redemption of Thieves ~ Book IV
Journey of Thieves ~ Book V
Rule of Thieves ~ Book VI

Catalysts of Chaos Series

Mistress of Masks ~ Book I
Betrayer of Blood ~ Book II
Summoner of Storms ~ Book III

Other Titles

Dreamer's Journey

Printed in Great Britain
by Amazon.co.uk, Ltd.,
Marston Gate.